The White Coyote

Books by Melissa McLarty

The White Coyote

Pieces of Tradition

The Metaphysics of Birth
(Release due date 2018)

Independently Published by McLarty Family

Melissa McLarty

The White Coyote
A Novella
The Laughing Owl Narrative Collection

The White Coyote
Part of a series in; The Laughing Owl Narrative Collection
Nocturnal Tales
Book #1
2014 by Melissa McLarty Copyright
Published By: Melissa McLarty in the house of McLarty Family Classics
Edited by: P.R.E Bastedo
   A debut story
All rights reserved under international copyright conventions. No part of this book may be reproduced or used in any manner whatsoever without prior written consent of the publisher, except in the case of brief quotations embodied in reviews.
Publisher's note: This book is a work of fiction. Names, characters, places and incidents either are the product of the author's imagination or used fictitiously. Any resemblance to actual persons, places, events, animals or locals is entirely coincidental.
Manufactured in Canada
Contact information:
MelissaMclarty34@Gmail.com
Library and Archives Canada Cataloguing in publication information is available.
USA ISBN numbers 1515348881   ISBN 13 9781515348887
Canadian ISBN numbers: 978-9948536-0-8   978-994536-1-5

Acknowledgements

This story is dedicated to everyone who loves the earth, with great hopes that you will be inspired to keep your hearts open to all the creatures we share this space with.

Thank you Jimmy, for telling me about the white coyote who made eye contact with you while you worked on a mine site. Tobin -Thank you for listening while I made up stories about where Jimmy's white coyote came from and critiquing my work as it progressed.

Chapter 1

The Arrival

The air has turned from crisp to gentle. Rays of sunshine float across our meadow. A few clouds in the sky funnel beams of light causing an amplified effect on newly green and long patches of canary grass. I can smell warm cedar wood on the air. In wisps the blades of grass cascade our meadow. Yellow and purple wild flowers speckle the landscape, moved gently by a soft breeze in a stark contrast to the fast flowing river edging this area. Wolves howl faintly in the distance.

I am perched high on a branch of the oldest pine tree inside the wide U shaped tree line bordering this meadow. From the large semicircle of forest up to the river's edge I can feel the air of this place breaths calmly. I hear butterflies fluttering their wings, and flitting about the open bright space in front of me. I smell fresh flowers blooming. Night is my domain and nothing can hinder my alertness of all surroundings even when the sun is shining. Have you guessed who I am?

From here, I can see with my eyes shut by hearing all things in the land. You may be asking how I do this? I will explain myself for you;

I am Laughing Owl, and I am the last one of my species. I have been both feared and revered since humans gave me my name. I am one of earth's oldest creatures. I can become nearly invisible, I fly silently, and I am the constant observer. Turning my head in all directions while keeping my body still, I miss nothing around me. I can pinpoint roots from any plant slowly growing beneath me and stretching new life through the dirt. My feathers help me feel the rhythm of a mouse's heart beat when I soar above him. When my shadow shades the sun from any prey beneath me, all things move faster until my prey is in my talon's grasp. If you sit with me quietly for a little while, I will tell you a story about my small friend the white coyote.

Today, White Coyote is under my perch on the outskirts of our meadow. I count the hairs on her hide before she knows I am above her. The air tickles her pearl fur as she sits on old pine needles covering the dirty forest floor. Shade from the trees does no good in camouflaging her. White Coyote may as well be in the middle of the meadow for her disability to hide among the greens, browns and golden sunlight penetrating our mountain valley. Long ago I heard a tail of a different white coyote that chose to die rather than soil his beautiful fur. Perhaps this little one sitting under me now is also that vain?
On the highest ridges of mountains surrounding the meadow, where snow never melts. That is the only place White Coyote blends in well. Once, last winter on the mountain peaks, an orange-brown coloured grizzly bear walked with in a paws length of where she sat. The bear did not know White Coyote was there. That day, as I watched from a tree hollow; I saw the thought cross White Coyote's mind of lunging from her snowy half-moon shaped resting position just to startle the bear. She had never heard of anyone who had surprised a bear before.
Today most animals have gathered in our meadow to watch a new species that has crept into our valley. For White Coyote, the new people do not appear threatening. They are slow moving and unaware of their surroundings. They seem to be concerned only with the river and straining out it's rocks through strange nests they have made. I know better than to be unconcerned with man's presence here. Men are wasteful and entitled just like bears or the wolves, all killing more fish and elk than they can eat, just because they can. Perhaps they do this so no one else can get any? The men pick plants in a way which destroys any chance of anything ever growing back. They soil the stream up water from where they work, camp and drink, causing all their filth and refuse to return to them and make them sick more often than not. Many men who have come to the mountains searching for gold have died from lack of understanding alone, leaving corpses so rotten not even the hungriest scavenger is interested.
Looking down, I see that White Coyote's tail sways nervously through the pine needles on our forest's floor. Looking out, I see

There is more to this new man than White Coyote will easily understand. Her head tilts hard to one side watching the intruders and hoping this angle will give her a better sense of why they do what they do. White Coyote remembers the day on the snowy mountain when she kept her place, allowing a great bear to pass her by. The thought gives her chills once more. Her pointed ears twitch back as the downy fur stretches across her sharp fangs. She smiles at the memory of her nearly brazen foolishness. Her laughter comes out in short barking screeches. I laugh along in harmonic howling hoots. We become hysterical at her imagined image of the great bear, scared out of his wits by one small lone coyote.
"Hissssssss."
Mountain Cat interrupts our happiness. Her tail twitches betraying her location low on her belly among the tall meadow grass otherwise she blends in perfectly. She scolds White Coyote.
"Be quiet you stupid dog, or you're going to attract the men into seeing the rest of us."
White Coyote lowers her head muttering. "What does it matter if they see us, I am not hiding?"
"And you couldn't hide even if you wanted to! Of all the pointless brainless creatures, you are by far the worst. Now shut up or they will take your too bright fur and wear it around their strange smooth bodies."
The thought of these clumsy pink men's bodies making it so quickly across the river, meadow and into the tree line where she sits before she can move, just to shake her out of her own skin causes White Coyote to laugh harder, cackling louder than she ever has before.
"That is ridiculous! You've lost your mind cat!" White Coyote continues on while howling hysterically. "Men can't move that fast! Besides they are busy with their strange pans shaking through the river's rocks looking for yellow stones."
The usually snappy Mountain Cat does not respond to White Coyote this time. Looking past the spot where Mountain Cat lays, White Coyote sees the men have stopped what they were doing and are now pointing in White Coyote's direction. Looking back to the cat, White Coyote sees she is gone.
"Cat?" White Coyote whispers feeling slightly fearful.

"Cat, if you're trying to frighten me, it has not worked. I have seen different men before too you know. Never this type though. I've seen the quiet and quick men who have arrows, but they are not hunting us now and most arrows cannot shoot this far even if the first people were here and of all the man types, Only Sasquatch is so fast and sneaky that he may catch any animal off guard. Birds, do you hear Cat's nonsense talk?"

But all the little birds are gone now too. And only the old pine tree stands still beside White Coyote. I stay perched on the branch pretending not to hear the foolish dog. Our meadow no longer breaths calmly with air and creatures as it had only moments ago. A chill comes to White Coyote, just the same as when she had almost scared the bear. Before White Coyote has time to decide on an action, her ears ring inside her head with alarm at the noise which surrounds her.

The old Pine Tree's bark splinters into pieces leaving a gaping hole in her trunk and shake the branch beneath me. I carefully and silently spread my long wings, correcting the jilt in my balance. The little coyote falls down unharmed and plays dead. Her heart beats quickly. Confidently a group of pinkish grey men walk towards us. They take long strides in scuffed, black leather boots. Marching through the meadow, they come within inches of a now invisible, crouching Mountain Cat- never knowing. All is silent except for the sounds of their feet crushing the grass beneath. A smell of excited sweat marking the men's foreheads is rancid to my nostrils. I slowly breathe out trying to displace the audacity of their strong scent. They are coming straight for us. We know how close they are with our eyes shut; still neither White Coyote or myself move the slightest muscle. We hear five men with five separate and distinct heart beats. The men's hand muscles strain in tension around their metal weapons.

Thése men are very close now. White Coyote now knows these men can kill her, with only the twitch of a finger. She lays motionless, foolishly hoping they do not see her. She understands their basic senses is all that moves them. She wishes her cackling bark had not caught their initial attention. Silently White Coyote calculates her

options, while allowing them to surround her lifeless looking and sprawled out body. The men's guns are drawn and aimed directly on White Coyote. One of the men nudges her with his boot. White Coyote's heart rate escalates but does not betray her. She remains still and limp. All five men breathe out in relief. They lower their guns. A large bearded man named Laurence, wearing a clean beige shirt hugging his bulging muscles speaks first. "Looks dead to me, eh." the handsome man's voice is friendly.
"Musta been a clean shot straight through the heart into this here tree. Nice shooting Laurence." A second smaller man speaks over the first while pounding the Pine Tree with a large callused hand.
"It's a pretty small wolf guys. You think it's still a pup?" a third man pipes in.
The fourth man stands back, dumbly trying to follow the conversation with his ears full of wax and his hands in his pockets. Laurence steps up to take over the scene.
"Nuff jibber jabben. Turn her over and check the entry point." Laurence throws his orders to the others, easily taking command. White Coyote bides her time, counting her heartbeat twenty to one in time with the men's. The largest man who spoke first, firmly grabs her hind paws. Spinning and lifting White Coyote counter clockwise, he exposes her soft vulnerable under belly. A look of confusion crosses all the men's faces as their subconscious collectively works in dumbfounded unison as if to silently scream 'There is no entry wound'. White Coyote's back is about to touch the pine needles beneath her. She uses the power from the large man turning herself against him. Diverting his energy around into a full lunge, she kicks him. She feels her back claws penetrate his chest. We smell the fresh trickles of blood staining the man's beige coloured, ripped shirt, as he falls to the ground. The men still standing around White Coyote do not register what is happening until it is too late for them to hinder her escape. She bounds through their legs chaotically before taking off in a full out run for the hills. Laurence draws his gun, but White Coyote is getting away, weaving through the trees. Laurence fires two shots and misses.

I stay where I am with unruffled feathers. I'm listening to the men beneath the old pine tree, as they collect themselves while trying to save face. The four men still standing pull their fallen friend up, off the ground.
"You're alright eh John?"
John dusts himself off, making light of his injuries. His blood gets hotter in his body. He is embarrassed to have been caught off guard. The heat inside him causes his scratches from White Coyote to leak blood faster. Turning more grey than pink, he sits back down on the ground, keeping his head up and doing his best to appear unscathed despite his obvious pain and fear.
"Just a coupla scratches by the looks of things John. You'll live to fight another day."
John offers a winced smile through his pain at the cooment, aware that all attention is now on him, and wanting to divert it away from himself and back to Laurence. He speaks only to lessen his condition. "That would've been a fine pelt, Laurence. Tough break."
"I've never seen anything like that. Outsmarted by a little wolf. Cunning little thing. Can't have that on the lose around camp." Laurence answers John, smiling back and not letting John off the hook.
John again forces a smile. In response he says "Next time shoot her twice Laurence.'
The men all laugh, but the laughter is insincere and meant only to ease growing tensions. Laurence offers his outstretched hand, helping John to get on his feet. Laurence supporting John as they slowly walk away. John is slightly hunched and becoming ever paler. Once the men get close to the river, I call after them with a few sharp screeching hoots.
      "Hoooohohoot!"
The men shiver. Their heart rates drop, hearing my cry. They do not turn back to see where I call to them from.
**

Immediately upon returning to camp, John takes a bad fever. One day turns into two days. He is not recovering, but getting worse. He Calls out for and has full conversations with a woman named Anya who is not here. As Sun sets on the third day, John's last breath leaves him. The tree begins to pass on too. The buckshot was too much for her three hundred year old bark and trunk. Her old limbs turn yellow and whither. We will never perch on that pine's high up branches again. The men bury their friend in our meadow under the shadow of the dying tree. Wiping sweat from their faces they throw the last of the disturbed dirt atop their fallen friend. Returning to camp, they drink whiskey, eat elk and talk around a crackling fire about how tough gold panning is in the Rocky Mountains. They name this spot where they have settled in "Hell" and whisper amongst themselves that it is damned here. White Coyote and I listen to the men from a safe distance tucked in this time, more securely amongst the trees and darkness. She wants the men to leave her territory. White Coyote senses the breaking of their will to stay. She cackles with malice towards the group. The men pick up their guns, however they know that White Coyote is too clever to come into their camp. She is only taunting them. Unfortunately for White Coyote, she does not understand how formidable the enemies she's made really are for this species of men- much like a parasite is not capable of living without destroying all signs of life around them. The fire at the men's camp burns through the night. In loud voices met by applause, the men boast to each other. "I will have that little wolf's hide for a coat!" Laurence vows.
"When Anya arrives I will give her John's claims as well as half of my own!" The quiet man makes a drunken pledge that sounds nice and at the same time is meaningless since every man knows a woman cannot work a claim.
The men continue on with John's wake, while composing plans to split their time evenly between finding their fortunes and killing any creature who threatens them.
The next day more men come. Everyday more and more men come until an entire cold season has passed. The men built large, warm wooden shelters for themselves across our meadow. The old pine's sister trees are gone now too.

Many birds do not return this year to our valley with the spring sun. The majority of wolves and other large predators have mostly been pushed far back too, now inhabiting a different valley further away. Only a small group of animals remain in this place with the men- too traumatized, injured or old to leave. All who stay have contracted this new man's morbid sickness and are now only able to survive by stealing what another creature holds dear or depending on scraps and crumbs left by the men. Symbiosis has died.
***
Having stopped panning the river with their hand bowls looking for shiny yellow stones the men now use a motorized moving slanted tree, which they have turned into a giant phallic machine. It dredges the river and sorts the rubble for them, taking only one thing and discarding all else into huge useless piles. It can't go on like this for long before they lay complete waste to the land. I suspect these men will move on to the next valley only once this place is depleted and rearranged in totality.

When the weather becomes very hot, the first people return as they have to this meadow for thousands of years. The gold hungry men learn from the first people the location of something called coal, but nothing else. They begin blowing holes in mountains, now looking for black coal rocks too. The first people do not like what the new men are doing to everything around the sacred meadow. Tension grows. The new men do not think things through. They kill some of the first men and give some of the first women babies. They build towns. New women come. They have more babies and with them come the bible carrying pastors. The first people get segregated to the eastern windiest areas of the valley. Although it is a sad life for the first people and their old women know the herbs to stop growth in a womb, they have never been wasteful in their ways, and they do not give up. The places for the first people are called reservations. Soon the new men need a train. They build a railway so they can take away more black rock from the mountain and bring in more new men.

White Coyote and I watch as the new men develop their schemes. We call to them. Taunting the men only when they cannot fully see us, letting them catch us in the corners of their eyes. The men make more vows to have the white pelt of the killer ghost dog. Over the time, Man has made every attempt to eradicate Mountain Cat's life, but he cannot catch her specifically because she is too quick. He did manage to kill Great Father Grizzly and now only the female and her young roam the hills around our valley. Most birds no longer even migrating over this area. Loud booms echo throughout our valley as the men burrow holes into the mountain, taking it down piece by piece. The men bring in weasels to eat the large rats that followed them on their trains. The weasels ravenous hunger can't stop at the rats. They eat almost all the small birds, lizards and snakes who had remained. The men and the weasels grow much too large and fat, but they keep going.

We, who are not man, talk amongst ourselves often. Bear, Bird, Fish and Cat. Plants, Moon, River and Sun. No one knows how to stop man without also hurting everyone else.

"Man is a menace, he will kill us all!" Robin sings as she glides past the animals that remain. "Man's weasels steal my eggs or eat all my chicks as soon as they hatch. I cannot keep pace with what they've brought on me. With the noise they make on the mountains, I will never find another mate. I can't move on."

All ears turn to beaver as he slaps his tail on a log in agreement with Robin. He speaks angrily.

"We are all moving on more quickly than we have in the years before man came, yet we go nowhere. The old genes are gone. Our young do not grow as strong and wise, only spry and weary. Look at where Old Pine Tree and her sisters once stood! In her place there's only thin divided saplings. Those saplings will never grow more than twenty feet high. Everything is shrinking and becoming diluted according to this new man's needs."

Long Horn Sheep bahs in disagreement, trying to calm the situation down."Nooooooo. Noooooo." Secretly the sheep don't understand what the fuss is about, and they do not really mind the noise, or the crowded mountain passes man has given them. The new smaller and more timid deer agree with the sheep. They do not mind what man has done to the valley. Their numbers have grown with man's development and help.

Standing up, Mother Bear growls from the hills.

"It may seem like more to sheep and other fools, but it is less. I know about what is most because bears need the most all the time. There is less good hunting and gathering land left every day. If I take anything in their land, they shoot at me. I cannot make it through the winter now without waking up early from hunger."
White Coyote listens quietly, but smirks and shakes her head at Bear's complaint. She remembers the old apple tree that she loved from years back. Bear had taken every last apple and seed from, than tore up the bark just to show everyone who did it. Bear is the only one that gets the luxury to destroy everything and sleep a full season while other things grow back. Coyote thinks Bear is just as selfish and greedy as the men.
Mountain Cat has been watching White Coyote and guesses now as the best time to attack the dog. Everything in the meadow wants blood today. Mountain Cat holds her own grudge from the day White Coyote drew the men here, with her careless laugh. Mountain Cat places blame on White Coyote for the rest of the men coming. Mountain Cat thinks it is White Coyote's fault her kitten that was trapped by the men's hunting dogs. Mountain Cat hates dogs.
"White Coyote brought the men too close. If we make her leave, the men will leave too." She whispers to the sheep.
"Yasssssss. Yassssssss! The sheep bah agreement. "It's White Coyote's fault. Make her leave."
Deer nods along with the large group of sheep. "Things will be safer for me without the Coyote."
Robin comes to us ready to sing the lasted news, but eyes me up suspiciously before retreating. I know that all other birds hate owls, however I have never personally threatened Robin.
"Someone has to go!" She chirps her new song to all creatures in the valley.
"I never have liked sharing my territory!" Bear roars, caught up in the group frenzy. Her giant paw pads toward the rock White Coyote is sitting on. "Leave!" Bear hollers while swiping at Coyote's face. Beaver sees this happening and he is frustrated. Beaver knows the original problem is not the little coyote. She has never bothered him. He decides she is not worth making a mortal enemy over. Quietly he swooshes away, retreating back into his den. Bear has always had

final say among the animals here. As long as Bear does not bother Beaver; Beaver will be okay.

Chapter 2
Exile

Bear's first swipe barely misses White Coyote's muzzle. Bear windmills her large paws while falling forward, grabbing and tearing out the skin on White Coyote's shoulder and side, attempting to regain balance. White Coyote turns tail, running and whimpering toward the mountains with her back rounded and tail between her legs.

Spastically, she darts sideways like a scared housecat expecting everything she encounters to lash out at her for no reason. White Coyote runs on adrenaline in this manner for days. She goes up hills, down hills and through new valleys, until she feels far enough away from the scene of attack and betrayal. White Coyote's legs give out beneath her. She curls into a shaking half ball that resembles the crescent moon above. Here in the open, she spends the night.

White Coyote cries out in her sleep. The sound is shrill much like a new born human child. I cannot comfort her. With empathy, I look down at her from my tree post hundreds of yards away. Many wolves have claimed this place as their territory. They hear her cries. White Coyote is afforded no rest, her twitching body spasms, jerking her eyes wide open she sees that she is now surrounded by a large hungry wolf pack closing in on where she has taken refuge. Scared, White Coyote jumps up. She runs, and runs until she has left them behind too.

Stopping, she stands still under the moonlight. Her paws bleed, her mouth hangs open, panting, from the strain of her adrenalin induced flight. White Coyote's brown eyes try to see in every direction, her large black pupils nervously shifting back and forth. In the distance, a pebble slides down a hill. This noise starts the high strung dog's twitching again. Startled by something insignificant, she runs further away. She keeps going, running on until her body will no longer move by her own free will.

Again she falls, collapsing in a heap; her lungs panting wildly. This new valley that I have followed her into is barren. She was easier to track here from the air than she would have been from land; making wild zigzags, jumping and dodging around erratically. This place is no good for White Coyote. The sun shines too hot in the day. A strong wind blows too fierce in the night. The dry grass on the ground cracks in surrender to the wind. Trees grow sparse with crooked trunks instead of proudly straight towards the sun. Any gusts of air will carry her resting cries far distances. I lift my wings upwards and out, cradling my neck with my shoulder bones in resistance to the harsh elements, as they try to blow and force me away from White Coyote.
But even the wind cannot move me unless I choose to take flight.
If White Coyote was smaller, I would mark her as my prey. Her injuries are deep and unclean. Bear has marked my little friend with filth and death. She has lost not only her home and her mind, but her will to live as well.
The sun rises, looking like a large pink and orange ball in the sky. All things living here come to life. White Coyote opens her sore eyes and curls her sad little body more tightly amongst itself. Her wounds are still open, but for lack of food and water the blood from her body has dried up. There is rapid movement the in the grass at this place. Small mites and ticks so insignificant no animal and not even the wind will bother with them have claimed this valley for their home. They feast on these trees so demented and beat down by the wind that the tiny bugs easily finish them off, rotting out the bark with hundreds of small nibbles. The mites and ticks have caught on to White Coyote's desperation as well. Their excitement grows at the prospect of a fresh meat feast. The bug's noise becomes a high-pitched hum only the best ears can hear.
Like the crooked, decrepit trees struggling to live around her, White Coyote's body withers in twisted pain. The sun offers her no nurture here in this place and instead burns her skin. The wind blows so hard at night and shakes her pain in further, giving her chills and shivers. A wave formed from thousands of parasitic mites comes out of the dry grass cascading into new homes for themselves on the shafts of White Coyotes once plush and beautiful coat.

The White Coyote 15

Only when the little bugs have stolen all nutrients from her fur, does today's sun set for the night. Many malevolent mites burrow within her skin. The mites live only for the next day, which awaits, so they can hatch more eggs. Restlessly, White Coyote dreams of her old valley, filled with rivers and the beautiful meadow she once called home. Sadly, her dreams give her no peace. She screams out in the night, waking to itches she cannot fully scratch. She knows she will never be able to return home.
Another and then another day pass, with both wind and insects tormenting the unmoving white coyote as she decays alive in the heat. Her mouth has become dryer than the dead, rough grass she lays on. Her tongue hangs long and outstretched. I can smell the rancid odor emanating from White Coyote, although I am not downwind. She drifts now between this world and the next. Her eyes half open are almost fully crusted over. I expect her to die soon. The images make me feel in a way I have never felt before. I look west towards the setting sun. Drawing back my head, I prepare to hoot a farewell song that will carry her spirit on to the next place. Perhaps then she will be at peace. Pushing my head forward, I open my beak. My own song does not come out of my mouth from within me. Out of my beak comes a sound that is the terrible cackling laugh of the White Coyote. This new sound startles me so badly that I almost fall off the twisted branch, which I am clinging to. Instead of guiding White Coyote into the next realm, she speaks through me- in silent whispers that echo to the core of my bones. She needs my help and will take away everything I am to survive.
"I am trying to help, and now is the time for you to embrace eternal silence. Be calm little one. Let go." My words do nothing to sooth her. She laughs loud and hard.
"Our bond cannot be broken so easily my wise old friend, go fetch us a mouse!"
I don't like her words in my head. I shake my body around violently rattling the tree attempting to displace this uninvited wandering spirit. White Coyote grasps me firmly with unseen force. I must obey her. I leave my perch on the tree, soaring forward. I am flying high towards a mountain peak. I race to catch the sun as it sets lower, downward, threatening to disappear forever into the night.

Flying high, I curve my flight downwards into a valley we have already crossed. This is where the wolves live. I hear a mouse rushing towards its little den. Diving downwards at the ground, I snare the mouse; its small neck breaks in my beak before it knows what happened to it. There is still dim light in the sky as I fly back fast with the little thing I've fetched. Returning to half dead White Coyote, I drop my lifeless mouse between White Coyote's open teeth. Her long, dry and outstretched tongue curls back as a wave upon the little mouse. She swallows it whole. The sun has set and the sky goes completely dark.

"More."

Her voice echoes through me in a way I cannot refuse. Ignoring her request is as possible as discounting the brightness of the sun, the darkness of night, or the wetness of rain. She and I continue on like this all evening long. With every rodent I fetch for her, my resistance to her pleas becomes weaker. I find myself regurgitating pellets from the indigestible remains of mice that I have not myself consumed. When the sun rises and White Coyote has had her fill, she stands on shaky legs. She moves slowly and limps towards the base of a close, crooked tree. This tree offers her no shade, and long ago ceased being able to grow leaves if it ever could at all. She chooses here to lay her body for the day. I perch directly above her on a far outstretched branch. I close my large all seeing owl eyes. I experience unconscious sleep, as I never have before.

The moon enters a night sky. I awake confused. Looking around, I see White Coyote lies still beneath me. She does not appear alert; she is dreaming but not gone from the land. I soar away from our twisted tree in search of more mice. I fetch many for White Coyote. We carry on like this for a long time. I lose all track of the sun and moon as well as my own needs. My feathers begin to molt. My once silent wings become loud on the breeze. Again White Coyote tells me what she wants.

"More"

She leaves me no leeway for my own thoughts or wants. I try to shake her presence off me, but she cackles her piercing laugh all the harder at my resistance. My only choice is to feed her until she becomes satisfied enough to release me back to my own accord.

The White Coyote

The wolves are coming. They have smelled opportunity in White Coyote's rotten mange flesh, all the way from their own valley. The wolves want to investigate what died. When they come, they will not stop to rest here. The damages and dangers of sleeping on this ground among the dead who are infested with mites are well known to the wolves. They approach our fried valley with slow moving caution. The females of this wolf pack have stayed behind in their own valley with their young, not risking exposure to the parasitic bugs that own our uninhabitable land. White Coyote is in better shape now to move. She will not hold her ground to face the pack of wolves approaching. White Coyote stands under the threat of immanent danger approaching. She tilts her head from side to side, getting her bearings and deciding what direction she can choose. "We are coming for you." The wolves' deep-throated whispers taunt us on the breeze.
Our old valley is behind us, and wolf territory is beside. They are closing in quickly. We have only two options in front of us. Straight ahead over the long range of mountain peaks or right towards the large sloping hills which lead to another windy valley that the First People were banished to years ago. As White Coyote starts to walk east, large clumps of bloody, matted, and mite infested fur fall from her emaciated body. Thick, dark and wrinkled skin is revealed on almost all parts of her mange body. Only her neck, top of her head, paws and tail still holds sparse tufts of full white fur. The moonlight illuminates the scars Bear had left along her side. The wolves howl loudly as they approach from the rear.
White Coyote moves straight forward very quickly. She reaches the top of a gentle rolling hill leading towards the Indian reservation. The wolves are too far behind her now to continue on her back, they will return to their own valley before it becomes too late for them too. A full moon peaks out from a large cloud, so brightly it appears that the cloud is behind it. Coyote laughs loudly at the moonlight.

Chapter 3
Kindness

White Coyote carefully circles the far edges outlining the reservation. It is difficult for her to accept. Seeing these humans, the First People, enclosed here in this way that is so different than it has been throughout all the world until now. In the past many different People would come together celebrating warm weather in the mountains. You used to be able hear children playing and people singing in a way that made every tree feel happy. You could smell fine herbs roasting with delicious bread and meat on open fires. Now, there is no smell and the people do not look as they used to with their flowing clothing and hair. The human's skin is lighter too. The sound of silence is prevalent, with only occasional interruption of the awkward jagged speech dictated from pink/grey coloured hands holding leather bound, brown books.

Where are the children?

The women who are outside sit silently in groups, going about their work sewing things for the townspeople to buy from them. The women's hair is worn short now and in severe angled bobs. White Coyote raises her snout into the air and cannot smell the tantalizing herbs and fire roasted meat that she had always associated with coming upon First People.

Who did this to my old friends?

In the past Wise Woman used to leave bones for White Coyote a small distance from their camp. Wise Woman would tell White Coyote to keep away the wolves who take everything, and the spirits that follow them. White Coyote would always oblige Wise Woman's request.

Is there a Wise Woman here?

I see a home slightly ajar from the rest of the houses on this reservation. I hear the crackling ambers of a small fire burning in the back of the home. It is a low fire, meant to be hidden. Only the slightest smoke escapes it. A woman with longer hair and darker

skin than the other people on the reservation exit's her little one
room home, walking around back. I leave my tree perch to better see
what this lady is doing. Silently I fly into the middle of the
reservation where most houses circle out. I land atop a large church
steeple, but I am still unable to see what is happening behind the
home. Wind changes direction and ever so slightly I smell the herbs,
rosemary and sage roasting. My ears hear faintly the small bubbling
sound coming from the fire behind the home. And then the smell is
gone again, even though wind has not changed direction this time.
White Coyote runs low and stealthy around the outside of town,
placing herself directly behind the interesting lady's back yard.
White Coyote is better able to hide from sight now that her
incandescent fur is mostly gone, however her bad mange smell
betrays her location to the smart lady tending the secret fire.
The lady sings out softly in a tone that White Coyote can understand.
*You have not come to me unexpected and I am not surprised you are
here. If you hold your place, I will give you a gift.*
White Coyote lays down patiently waiting and curiously watching
the lady with beautiful long thick black hair blowing in the ever
changing wind. The lady quickly removes a large stone from atop
her little fire using two long sticks. A delicious smell fragments the
air. White Coyote's mouth becomes moist. Assuming this is the gift,
she slowly creeps closer. The lady is aware of the dog's intentions.
She sings out again causing White Coyote to stop before
encroaching further onto the small cleared yard.
The lady pokes a stick into the hot creation cooking on the little fire.
She lifts out a white and green speckled oblong ball, now impaled by
the stick clear from the heat. She quickly wraps the delicious mound
safely into a blanket, while kicking dirt over her fire smothering it.
All smoke and smells immediately cease. White Coyote whimpers
softly, but the lady does not respond to the dog's groaning. The lady
carries her new blanket bundle of bread like most women carry a
baby around and into the front of her home. Shutting the door behind
herself, she disappears for a short time.
I take off, flying away from the church steeple and towards the tree
branch atop of where White Coyote lays waiting for the lady. Some

The White Coyote 21

of the people living at this reservation see me. They raise their heads slightly and squint. No one calls out greetings to me as the free First People who I met in the past had. A woman with the shortest hair, and perfectly tailored clothes worn in the new man fashion takes special notice of me; more than the rest of the women sewing in the fresh air. The attention does not appear friendly. Getting up from the rest of the group, she follows my path to the home where White Coyote waits. Instead of cutting around to the back after me, the woman squares herself to the front of the lady's home and marches towards the door. She knocks loudly three times. Without receiving an answer, she swings open the door and almost crashes it into the interior wall of the home.

A wonderful smell of fresh bread escapes out the open door causing some of the older women busy at their work sewing to smile softly and nod. White Coyote sneaks closer to the home, hoping the uninvited guest does not take all the food. A low snarly growl escapes White Coyote's hungry drooling mouth. The guest women has a smell about her like the man who shot at White Coyote long ago. We hear the lady singing slowly from inside her home. Her song has more than one purpose. It calms us and slows the fast angry heart of the new guest inside.

"You cannot make bread in the old way! It is not allowed. You will get us all trouble!" The guest speaks harshly trying to interrupt the rhythm of lady's song.

But the lady continues singing for a few more moments until she is ready to speak.

"Be calm." She says in the old language.

"You are crazy! You must speak English! I know you can do it better than any of us. Holding onto the old ways will only cause conflict and pain. The time you are in has past."

The lady responds only by cutting into the fresh bread. We smell the aroma escape from her little chimney in the roof. We hear a piece of bread being pushed forward toward the guest in an offering. The guest refuses. Huffing she loudly turns her nose up and walks back out the door she came in slamming it behind her. She stomps fiercely away from the home towards the group of women who are still sewing.

"You will not believe what that crazy old lady is up to now!" The women spews her new gossip to the others. We stop focusing on her, returning our interests back to the lady with the gift.

From inside the home, we hear the lady laughing in a way that holds more pity than humor.

This new spirit of boastfulness and waste has taken a strong hold of some, more so than others.

The lady does not forsake everything from her home that the new man has brought with him. Since men made the hunting grounds off limits, animal fat to moisten bread has been scarce. The missionaries have given the lady butter. Butter is not a bad thing in place of lard. She breaths in while touching her cooking. The lady lets her nose, fingers, eyes and mouth prepare her stomach for the good things coming. This lady will not be sharing her bread with the decrepit little coyote who awaits her outside.

I will not trap this animal in that way. If the White Coyote were to try this bread, it would never leave to live its life purpose. A white coyote may become a nice pet for a short time, however the bad of feeding a starving dog outweighs the good.

Her reasoning leads the lady to befriend White Coyote in a way that will not interfere with the creature's purpose. She rustles through her home. She has managed to save some old treasures, not yet plumaged from her by the new man. High on a shelf, she finds an old dusty package her grandmother had given her long ago. It's a small piece of white and black striped horse skin. It's tied shut with special woven twine. This package holds inside it about forty large black seeds. The lady empties half the seeds into her hand and crumples a tiny piece of bread on top. Opening the back shutter of her home, she tosses the tiny breadcrumbs and seeds into the wind. She screeches out, low in a friendly owl call to signal me. I fly down from my tree branch perch, collecting crumbs and seeds into my stomach. While I do this, the lady sings to White Coyote of a place about a one-day walk from here that is between two hills. White Coyote listens with perked ears to the lady. I do not take all the seeds and once I have gathered up most of them, I fly away.

White Coyote bows her head to the lady then follows me further east.
**
This land is sacred. It does not look special to pass it by, however anyone who spends much time here will see what is special about it. Plats grow faster, stronger and greener than normal here. The sun shines just right and there is a small cave opening half way up the south hill, which only the most astute would see. Here between the hills, is what looks like a normal pond and it is not normal. The waters come from deep within our earth, pooling here gently between the two hills. Birch Trees grow straight and tall, maintaining their greens leaves longer than any other before the fall turns them crimson red and causes all leaves to drop. Little mice make homes for themselves free of any fear, they nestle in the roots of these great trees. Sparrows, Robins and Blue Jays busy themselves singing their sweet melodies. They have built many nests here. A crow watches from the distance, and chooses to leave this beautiful place when she sees me approach.
A great number of rabbits live here, making dens for themselves. The rabbits must've driven out the weasels that came with the new men years ago by their numbers alone. Although these rabbits are wise, they do not yet know that they should fear White Coyote and I. They sit curiously on their fuzzy haunches as we approach, noses twitching with large dark gentle eyes.
Immediately White Coyote and I take one rabbit each. Our kills are fast and almost discreet, yet not discreet enough for the rabbits' behavior to continue on in their carefree fashion. They take to their holes, silently peering up at us with fast beating heats.
There are large fish in the small pond. I can hear them moving under water in the deepest middle. White Coyote is curious about the fish too. She tilts her head trying to hear what swims beneath the ripples, but her hearing is not as good as mine. She turns her body backwards, away from the pond and flicks a leaf using her paw into the edge of the water. A great rainbow of scales becomes visible swishing to investigate what disturbed the previously glass surface. White Coyote does this again and again. Trying each time to turn her head fast enough to glimpse the swimming creature moving behind

her. But the fish do not stay visible long enough to allow White Coyote a good look. She decides to wait and see. With her belly full of rabbit she lays down, crossing her paws in front and quietly watches the pond.

A frog hops trustingly close to White Coyote. The frog is interested in checking out the leaves in the water, he hopes little bugs are trapped between the foliage and the surface. He sticks out his frog tongue in anticipation, licking his thin frog lips. He jumps forward enthusiastically. The dip from the slight incline where White Coyote lays, leading to the water's edge gets the best of the frog in his excitement. His long green legs catapult him further than he had originally anticipated to go. Straight into the wetness.

White Coyote laughs as the awkward little frog flails, sinks and sprawls out his tiny hands, taking in the surprising water and grasping towards the surface air. White Coyote sits forward and leans closer towards the pond, wanting a better vantage point to observe the silly creature.

White Coyote catches her reflection rippled through the pond's water and she frightens herself. Pulling her upper lip back, she growls. The image scares her more. With her tail between her legs, she jumps backward. I hoot in laughter at her shock, but she ignores me completely. Slowly she creeps directly to the water's edge and peers down at the horrid presence beneath her. She has forgotten all about the silly frog. Sniffing, she stares down at the grotesque dog beneath her. It has a very faint smell like a wolf in the distance. It does not make any sound as its mouth opens in a warning bark, cruelly mimicking her. White Coyote tilts her head while perking her ears forward, trying to make sense of the highly strange creature in front of her. It does the same thing. White Coyote backs up. It disappears. She peeks back at the water and it reappears. White Coyote concludes the thing to be a water dog, confined to the depth of the pond. To test theory she dips one paw into the pond. The other dog reaches for her at the same time. Timidly she breaks the water's surface, and the anomaly disappears.

The increase in movement has attracted a large fish to the surface. It goes after the frog trying to pull himself onto a leaf. White Coyote

pounces full steam into the pond, landing with her jaws clasped around the fish's spine. It fights her with all its might. She mistakes the fish's strength for the mysterious ugly water dog. She thinks it also fights her for the fish. This frightens White Coyote terribly. She scrambles to get back on land safely. Jumping out of the pond, she does not shake off. She moves sideways with her back hunched and her shackles up. A low cry staggering deeply from her throat. She can't take her eyes off the spot where that monster stole her fish. The surprise fight was much too great for any fish, weather attacked by one dog or two- the fish bobs lifelessly at the surface. White Coyote watches the fish, thinking the ugly, monster dog must be trying to bait her while her thoughts run wild;
No dog in it's right mind would give up such a nice meal so easily.
The fish floats closer towards the shore, becoming almost banked. Still terrified of the water dog, White Coyote reaches out a bald shaking paw. She attempts to pull the fish onto safe land. The water dog also reaches for her fish. White Coyote lets out a scream, pulling her paw back in close to her own body. Mustering all determination, she reaches out again, this time looking away and unable to bare the horrible site mimicking her every move.
Success! She gracelessly pulls the fish onto shore. Cowering, she takes it in her watering mouth and backs away until the pond looks smaller than me. Here at a safe distance White Coyote drops her fish onto the dry grassy ground. She feels a happy light heartedness that she has not felt since the old valley.
This shining rainbow fish is the best thing in the world!
White Coyote drops her head to the side and roles over the fish, squishing its' fatty, oily juices into her aching skin. With her paws to the sky, White Coyote shimmies her back into the fish, feeling so happy. She jumps up excitedly looking lovingly at her squished up, rolled on fish. She pounces at the fish a couple of times with her front paws. She takes a few steps back from it, almost dancing with joy. She admires the treasure with her round brown eyes. Springing forward, she pounces the lifeless fish again, grabbing it up in her jaw. She flicks it forward, spinning the fish head over tail in front her. She chases it, as the thing spirals through the air. The fish lands too close to the pond's edge.

White Coyote growls, letting the dead fish know there is no escape this time. She snatches it up between her teeth and goes running around the small pond three times in victory. Finally, White Coyote comes to a full stop, holding the fish in her drooling mouth. She lays down in the same spot where she had first been to observe the water. Making herself comfortable and keeping a firm eye on the pond, White Coyote noisily devours her catch. Eyes from inside the cave, and another pair just beyond the hill are observing her. Not noticing, she eats every morsel of the fish; tail, bones and all. Only the shiny scales remain outside of her stomach. The fish scales are stuck to her rotten mange skin. She shines in the sunlight. Realizing she is thirsty, White Coyote works up the courage to approach the pond for a drink. Looking down this time, she sees a friendlier beautifully sparkling dog. She likes this fish dog a lot better than the first water dog she saw. She does not feel threatened by its glittering demeanor. Fish Dog is only thirsty too; there is enough water in the pond that they can share.

Feeling very satisfied with herself and somewhat exhausted, White Coyote smells the air, trying to determine a suitable place to dig a den. The slight odor of wolf is still in the breeze. A rabbit runs towards a small hole near a large birch tree. White Coyote lunges at the rabbit, only an attempt to frighten the small creature and usurp his hole. She is too big for the rabbit's den but this hole will be a good start. Frightened, the rabbit runs away. White Coyote begins digging.

I fly down from where I perch and break the scared rabbit's neck using my strong beak. I do not soar off with my large catch; I begin to slowly swallow it whole on the ground. White Coyote stops digging and sets eyes on me. I look back into her eyes. She resumes her den making.

Once White Coyote has cleared enough dirt so that the hole is slightly larger than her body, she tucks into it and collapses in deep, content sleep. I regurgitate pellets of indigestible rabbit remains along with the black seeds from the Wise Woman onto the freshly dug dirt. I spend the rest of my evening making Crows old nest into my new home, lining the nest with my molten down feathers. I search out pretty things that I may like to place around it.

The White Coyote

I catch a few mice, as the sun rises for a new day. Feeling full, I slip into my usual ever alert sleep.
***
I dream of dragons and unicorns from the days when I was not the oldest and wisest of creatures on the earth. They soar above me and dance below me. Pixies and pretty fairies flit around my nest catching me up in their spells so that I cannot eat them. This is a beautiful place. It hold long forgotten magic of lovely hopes and dreams. The wise woman was kind to send us here. Last night was the first of many which White Coyote does not cry out in her sleep. I feel light and peaceful. I hear little mice busying themselves on the ground beneath me. Two trees over, a robin feeds her young chicks in their nest. The robins here have had no reason yet to become weary of my presence and this sweet mother bird's calm radiates in all directions.

Chapter 4
A Cold Winter

I sense heartbeats coming from the cave dwellers who live beneath us. Their hearts are larger than anything I have encountered in the past. The rhythm that comes from them feels long, low and slow. I'm yet to catch them with my eyes. They're better at being invisible than me. They are intrigued with a new fruit growing around their home on curling vines. I can tell you; by the sounds of their movements, these beings have thin waists and long limbs like the skinny melon vines grown from the seeds Wise women gave us. White Coyote's den is covered over with the spiraling vine barring fruit.

The cave dwellers dig a tunnel under White Coyote's den. The melon plant's vines now grow downward through the dirt and into the caves, as well as upward towards the sun and around White Coyote's home. I hear the cave dwellers storing melons that sprout underground. As if they are preparing for something or someone. The nights are getting colder against White Coyote's bare mange skin. The extra foliage from the melon vines offers White Coyote cover while inside her den, but little warmth. Large plump green and pink melons sprout daily on the vines. White Coyote likes eating this fruit even better than fish. At night the cave dwellers sneak above ground. They secretly watch White Coyote while she sleeps and creep around her in their strange way, never coming close enough that White Coyote might catch them if she wakes.

During the night White Coyote dreams of when she was a small pup with her parents and siblings. Her dreams progress and she becomes more like her mother. The odor of a lone wolf grows daily on the breeze surrounding our new home. The lone wolf who watches White Coyote from a distance is an omega. The Alpha of his pack ran him off in the last Valley. He is displaced from his original group. He has tracked White Coyote here hoping to find a mate.

White Coyote does not appear concerned by the lone wolf lingering on our outskirts. She has marked this place as her own and she is happy here. The lone male wolf does not pose a threat upon White Coyote's territory, fish or melons. He is unlike the waterdogs living in this pond who drive White Coyote crazy. White Coyote is curious about the Wolf's scent. His smell does not repulse her.

The pond is growing very cold. Fish no longer approach its icy surface. White Coyote foolishly blames the water dogs for the lack of fish. The frogs are sleeping now, too deeply in the ground for big fish to catch. The little birds have left this place, taking their grown chicks flying south. Mice have gone underground, and are lost to me for this season. The melons on White Coyotes plant become hard and cold as rocks at night. In the daylight sun, the melons shrivel and rot away. This will be a harsh place to spend winter. As the three stars that humans call Orion's belt become center of the night sky, the earth becomes frozen. I take dry leaves from the birch tree to build up my nest against the growing cold. Crow laughs at me and my efforts from the distance.

White Coyote shivers at night. The den she dug with care will not protect her through this winter. The extreme cold makes travel impossible. White Coyote cannot move away from her home on the edge of the pond. Having balding, sparse fur is new for White Coyote, in winters past, her coat always kept her warm. Although White Coyote's mange skin is thick, it will not work as a barrier against the frost.

The sun rises today shining light over the northern hill. A lone male wolf sleeps out in the open. His grey double down coat keeps him hot at all times. Yesterday the lone wolf marked a large circle around this place as his territory. His big strong paws allow him to dig deep enough into the hard ground that Its easy for him to find rabbits, ground hogs and sleepy mice. While White Coyote wastes away again, Lone Wolf grows stronger bolder.

Night sets in. The air is hard and cold. Orion's belt is not yet at the highest point in this evening's starry sky. Looking up into the sparkling abyss, White Coyote understands that things are going to become worse before they get better. Bear gave her a death sentence by tearing away her fur.

The White Coyote

The mange will kill White Coyote this winter. White Coyote shivers, in an attempt to shake away these morbid thoughts that attack her. A full moon appears in the sky from behind a cloud.
Lone Wolf howls at the moon. He is howling to White Coyote, letting her know he is here and this place is theirs. He wants to go to her down by the pond, but does not know the best way to approach her. When he was a pup, and his father was away hunting Lone Wolf witnessed a dog foolish enough to approach his mother's den. When the stray dog came at his mother from behind, she pretended not to sense the outsider's presence. When the stray became close enough to mount his mother she turned, teeth bared and tore the intruders throat out. When father had finally come back with the rest of his hunting pack, they ate the remains and buried the intruder's bones. Lone Wolf does not smell another male's presence here. He has seen no signs that White Coyote has a mate or pups of her own. From his experience, female dogs with pups could be more dangerous and unpredictable than man with guns. Bitches can appear accepting of an advance. They could even invite it. Without warning they could change their minds at the last moment choosing to attack. All wild females are cunning and aloof. Lone Wolf is not sleeping tonight. He lays awake, staring at the stars and moon in the sky. He wishes for a non-threatening way to approach the white coyote. A rabbit hops past him, giving the lone wolf an idea.
**
A sweet looking grey wolf face appears in White Coyote's line of site. He is peering down at her from atop a hill. His handsome face peeking around a large birch tree trunk. His blue eyes slightly narrowed in a friendly manner, he holds a rabbit between his big smiling teeth. The sly wolf stays still like this for a few moments. He wants acknowledgement that White Coyote sees him and desires what he has. White Coyote realizes the wolf is not going away, she crouches low on the cold ground staring up at him growling and shaking. Lone Wolf approaches her from the front, slowly. When he is only a few feet from White Coyote, she growls louder. This lets him know not to move in any closer. Lone Wolf flicks the dead rabbit in her direction. White Coyote catches it midair, quickly devouring it while at the same time keeping one eye on the wolf.

White Coyote is starving. She devours the rabbit, finishing it completely, she snarls and backs up. Lone Wolf stays where he is. The two hold eye contact for a few moments before the big wolf turns in polite retreat back behind the hill he came from.
Lone Wolf brings more rabbits and mice at night. He brings enough that I can have some too. I watch them in this careful courtship. Never did I ever believe a day might come where Id gratefully be taking a coyote's cast offs, however, I find the extra mice non offensive in every way. The air is too cold for me to go flying about in search of prey I will not find. This is the time of year that I stay as still as possible. My body does not move properly or stealthy through the frozen, ice cold air. Easy extra nourishment is welcome. Weeks pass like this, with Lone Wolf bringing his bribes. Every gift gets him closer to White Coyote and he holds her gaze longer now. He wags his tail as he walks down the hill. White Coyote still growls when he comes too close too quickly. At night, Lone Wolf sleeps atop the hill and watches White Coyote shivering in her shallow den. He has all the patience in the world, but he is concerned about how much longer the little female will survive on her own. She cries out in her restless cold sleep. Lone Wolf longs to go to her. He wants to comfort her and warm her with his heater fur. He wants to put pups into her emancipated frame and make her look as full as he thinks she should be. He does not notice the secret cave beings who live here too, they observe him and plan out his fate while he plans the fate of White Coyote.
Concerned about the cold on his potential mates` bare skin, Lone Wolf gathers the scattered rabbit and mice hides strewn about the pond. He brings them to the foot of White Coyote's den. He enters and digs it out larger. He packs the newly made space with the furs from his kills. He had seen his mother and sisters do this in the past when preparing for puppies. Lone Wolf thinks that White Coyote should be doing these things for herself, but he knows she is a strange sort of creature and no proper wolf. He decides to treat her as mother would a beloved runt pup. White Coyote lays staring at the ice-covered pond annoyed and pretending to pay no notice to the large wolf messing about with her den.
Tonight White Coyote sleeps soundly surrounded by rabbit furs.

The White Coyote

Lone Wolf watches down on White Coyote's den while lying atop the north hill. His efforts will help the mange female coyote make it through another cold night. A rabbit hops merrily across Lone Wolf's path. It comes to a quick end as he devours it. He smiles a wolfy grin…
I am close to being satisfied. He thinks to himself.
The sun appears over the east mountain peak. Lone Wolf brings White Coyote another fresh kill. He takes his usual path down the hill. He weaves clumsily with big jaunty paws through the birch trees. He comes within feet of White Coyote, dropping the rabbit. She growls but he does not retreat. He makes no effort to show her that she may take his gift easily.
Holding his stand, he looks deeply into White Coyote's weary, shifting eyes. Lone Wolf attempts to smile. His smile has the opposite affect he had intended, it causes White Coyote to bear her teeth and growl lowly in return. Undaunted Lone Wolf holds his place. Staring at White Coyote, he returns her growl in a lighter manner while hopping from side to side in a playful way. This works. White Coyote smiles and pounces toward him. She fakes him out, pretending to go left but at the last moment cutting right, snatching the rabbit carcass from him. White Coyote runs around the pound wildly. Jumping and prancing she throws the rabbit into the air and catches it again with a snap of her jaw. Lone Wolf chases her, gently nipping at her hind legs while she runs. He is faster than her, and a lot stronger too, but does not let White Coyote feel this fact.
White Coyote drops the dead rabbit and Lone Wolf takes it from under her paws. She now chases him around the pound. He lets her catch him, and concedes the rabbit back to her. He chases her in circles until she becomes exhausted. She lies down to eat the hard earned meal. Lone Wolf retreats to the hills, returning a few hours later with another rabbit. This time he tears it down the middle. Allowing White Coyote to take the smaller half, he devours his share beside her. When their bellies are full he inches closer towards her. She does not growl at him. He feels brave. He places his large furry grey paw atop her small bald paw. They sit this way for a little while. Lone Wolf leans in and licks White Coyote's face.

She rolls her body towards his and they snuggle. Gently she kisses his snout. The full moon gets high in the sky. Both dogs retreat to White Coyote's rabbit fur lined den for the evening. Orion's belt glitters among all the stars above them throughout the night. Exhausted from their evening together, the two dogs sleep soundly inside the den. White Coyote and the grey wolf do not hear the group of men slowly approaching them from outside. All over this land the same is happening. It's dangerous everywhere, the new men constantly encroach more and more space, they are the reason owls like me have never let our guard down for too long. I hear them in the proceeding hills boasting about their gold finding expertise. The men are hatching plans while almost everyone else in the mountains sleeps. For them, the gold surrounding this pond holds more value out of the ground. Any one of these men will trade all the gold here for some quickly fading material thing, which they will use to impress easily fooled girls. Eventually the gold will end up in some distant location where it benefits only kings and queens. Their ways are corrupt. They will never allow anything considered valuable to remain underground, or untouched by their filthy greedy hands. They are too ignorant to understand the destruction they cause to our beautiful places is an action they will ever be able to restore.

The men are searching for areas that remain greenest throughout the coldest parts of winter. This anomaly lets them know where gold hides. Closer now, the men set their sites upon our little sanctuary. The healthy trees are exactly what the gold hungry eyes of the men had wanted to feast upon. These men could never be satisfied by only looking at this place. As days pass the men surround the pond, while newly sprouting wolf pups grow inside White Coyote's little womb. They begin to weigh her down heavier than nature intended. Lone Wolf has been such a good provider and White Coyote has grown fat from his gifts. Even if White Coyote could escape the destruction men have in store for this place, she will be unable to survive far from her den. White Coyote and the grey wolf are cornered together, trapped inside their little den. Outside, there are a lot of men who are setting up explosives. The men will bust these hills down piece by piece, and leave nothing but rubble behind them.

Chapter 5
The Underground

Grey Wolf lays with White Coyote, watching feet clad in leather boots shuffle past the small opening of their little den home. He growls, wanting to go out and defend his territory. White Coyote is scared. She convinces Grey Wolf that it will be better to stay hidden in their den for the time being. The snuggled pairs' hearts beat more quickly with every blast and footstep heard around them. Both dogs know it is only a matter of time before they are discovered or blown up. Constantly fearing that his mate and he will be aimed at specifically by the men's loud weapons causes Grey Wolf's mind to snap. He digs, pants and circles inside their small den incessantly. When he is not moving, he begins having very dark thoughts.
I can kill her and offer her corpse to the men; if I help them maybe they will let me go.
It is difficult for White Coyote to remain silently inside the den with Grey Wolf. She spends the majority of her time pretending to be asleep. The threat from this highly stressed wolf losing his mind while crammed beside her is no greater danger than the other terrifying events now overwhelming White Coyotes every waking moment. Explosions happen closer and louder every day around White Coyote. White Coyote does not lose hope, wishing they could both be someplace far away together. Wasting away, cornered and starving, the pair become thin. Grey Wolf's hunger is ravenous. The men do not give Grey Wolf or White Coyote an opportunity to leave. Day and night the men linger outside the den, standing proudly in their big boots and unknowing of the wolf beneath them. The men's only concern is of other men like themselves coming here to steal these riches which they have staked claim to as their own.
I should eat this coyote. Grey Wolf violently shifts between thoughts of harming White Coyote and wishing to protect her. His better nature is still strong enough to win this internal battle before he acts badly, however, every day he becomes weaker.

The fight inside him is almost completely gone. Grey Wolf and White Coyote's breath becomes slower. Their heart rates relax at irregular times and the once growing, wriggling pups inside White Coyote's belly become nearly still. All hope seems to be lost. They will starve and perish here in this used to be enchanted place. Lone Wolf strokes White Coyote's neck weakly with his dry tongue. White Coyote takes this as affection and nestles the top of her head into the side of her companion's shoulder, stretching out and exposing her vulnerable throat to the wolf.
**
A hole in the dirt opens beneath the pair. They fall through the ground into the caverns of the cave dwellers. Getting their paws back beneath themselves, White Coyote and Grey Wolf shake dirt from their fur. Looking around they notice the cave is faintly lit. There is a light at the end of this tunnel. Lush watermelons growing in all directions line its walls. They begin to eat the watermelons and both dogs agree that this is the best thing they've ever tasted. A strange noise beckons the two further down this cavern, towards the light. White Coyote struggles to walk. Lone Wolf does not rush ahead but keeps pace with her. He is distrustful of this new place that smells only of food.
The pair approaches the light at the end of this watermelon filled tunnel beneath their den. They come to an opening at the end. Looking forward, White Coyote can see this place is larger than her original meadow was. It takes her eyes a few minutes to adjust to the newness. Lone Wolf's hackles are up, with his stomach now full of watermelon, he is ready to fight to protect his female and their tiny growing pups inside her. He is confused about how he got to this place. He does not know what will come next. White Coyote moves further forward bravely. Behind her, Grey Wolf is crouching low, he feels worried and unsure; Ready to turn tail and bolt quickly back towards the den. He cannot leave because he knows that nothing but death awaits him by retracing his steps backwards. The ground shakes violently above them. The watermelon tunnel begins to collapse all around Grey Wolf. Reluctantly, he moves ahead. While thinking;

I don't belong here.
****

Above ground, from my nest, I watch the men bring in red sticks. These men are boastful and laughing. Full of pride for their newly found riches. They do not realize how vital this pond had been to life before their arrival. I have seen these red sticks before, loud and destructive. The sound the sticks make once lit hurts my ears. I seek cover in the only safe place I can see away from them. The dark cave on the south hill. I enter it and drop down wards at a severe angle. There is barely enough room to spread my wings. The cave's rock walls open and give way to a strange underground, serene space. I hold myself in a hover, allowing my eyes to adjust in the dim light and searching for a place to hide myself while I make a decent observation of what I've gotten into. I don't know how the cave dwellers maintain their secret life and space.
Here, large butterflies flit every which way. Some have purple wings and others' wings are bright orange. The air is as fresh and sweet as a spring mountain breeze. Flowers, berries and trees grow upside down from the dirt, rock and crystal-cracked ceiling. The floor is white gold and silver. Light reflects and shimmers in all directions. Deep streams with rainbow fish cross the precious metal floor. Drastic water falls edged by black rocks and lightly flowing lava line the vertical walls of this huge cavern. I hear the sound of a faint heartbeat echoing around this space. Gold stairs lead up to catwalks under the ceiling's foliage. Rain and dew drip down to the floor and flow towards the streams.
Grey Wolf lets out a large sigh, relaxing he sees nothing in this place is a threat. White Coyote is happy to have shelter and food cozily surrounding her. Looking down at them, from my perch right side up on an upside-down tree, I also feel good. This place in much better for spending the winter than where we were. I crunch a purple butterfly between my beak. It tastes good and wriggles as I swallow it whole. White Coyote and Grey Wolf walk towards the edge of a slow flowing, deep underground stream. Wanting to catch a fish for White Coyote; Grey Wolf dips his large front paw into the clean, clear and slowly flowing water, but he has no luck. All the fish quickly avoid him.

The White Coyote

White Coyote was always better at hunting fish anyways, so she catches dinner and shares it equally with her mate. She is feeling better now that her stomach is full and she is away from the loud noises that men cause in the outside world.
Grey Wolf sleeps and White Coyote is too curious for rest. Looking into the stream, she sees no reflection, only a large, jagged and speckled rock. Confused she tilts her head. The rock snaps at her playfully. White Coyote realizes it is not a rock, but an old snapping turtle. She flicks a piece of her fish towards the turtle in the stream. It swallows the snack and jumps up from the water onto the golden floor in front of White Coyote. Grey Wolf is so startled by the things sudden movement that wakes and he falls into the stream.
"I don't usually eat meat when I am underground, but a gift is a gift." The turtle's voice is both assertive and kind.
"There is nothing slow about you, even though you look like a rock." White Coyote laughs while speaking to her new friend.
Gulping, Grey Wolf tries to casually climb out of the stream, however he looks sheepish shaking himself off. Water flies all over Turtle, and White Coyote. Droplets hit me up on the tree branch. I spread my wings to let the beads drip from my feathers back to the three beneath. White Coyote shakes the excess beads off herself and Turtle slips back into the stream.
In the underground, we cannot see the sun or moon. Time passes differently here- not slower or faster but as if time is no real thing at all. True darkness never sets in. The waterfalls and the streams sparkle, as does the ceiling and floor. We eat whenever we are hungry and we rest when our stomachs are full. The cave dwellers who call this place their permanent home never approach us directly. In my dreams they tell me we are welcome here for as long as we wish to stay. In our dreams, the cave dwellers teach us the importance of storing food, that will last throughout the long winters. The cave dwellers hate the new man and what he is doing to the outside world, the only weapon they have is closing off this place of refuge to him. They say many years ago a great frost came and they helped the humans who dwelled above ground. This is why their waists are so thin, because they shared all they had.
*****

Sitting together by the stream, Turtle tells White Coyote the story about how she found herself underground.
"Long ago and far away, I had only heard of the ones who made this place in whispers. You know how it was; you'd catch glimpses of them from the corners of your eyes…
One day, I was sunbathing on a beach. I am very old now and yet I was not young back then. The sand started to feel hot beneath me, and my shell became very warm. Thinking I was an actual rock, one of them sat on my back. He quickly realized who I was, because I snapped at him and said "Get off my back!"
He became terribly embarrassed for having sat on me. Begging my pardon, he told me that if I followed the great whales, I too could use the underground streams and water falls in circumnavigating the earth.
The ones responsible for things here are a kind type who are well meaning. Their underground tunnels connect every corner of this world. If I had not met one, I would still be stuck on that beach today. Although it was nice in the sun, I like to move around too much to stay in one place like a rock forever."
******

Flying around this cavern while chasing the beautiful butterflies is fun. A dragonfly zooms past me, diverting me from the game I have made up. I follow the dragonfly towards a dark corner of the cavern that I had not noticed before just now. Here tiny mushrooms grow illuminating themselves in the shade. They whisper; "Eat me."
So I do, and now I can see the cave dwellers who look like a mix between ants and people.
"Do not get lost here." They whisper this to me.
"The world still has a need for laughing owls."
****

White Coyote grows very large. She is close to birthing her pups. The ant people surround her. Grey Wolf isn't able to see them.
"The time has come." The ant people say.
White Coyote howls out releasing her pain. A puppy appears, but he is all grey and has no life. The ant people take him away from the still laboring mother. White Coyote cries out after them, her heart is breaking.

The White Coyote

The ant people answer White Coyote's begging gently. "The first pup born must stay here with us. We will take good care of him forever."
"No!" White Coyote screams.
"That is how it must be, you will have another and you must focus on that for now." The ant people whisper softly to White Coyote as they stroke her head. This helps her feel calm.
The second pup comes without pain and takes its first breath of air immediately upon entering the world; she is extremely small but healthy and thriving. She looks like a littler, fuzzier version of how her mother used to be.
The ant people bury the grey pup into the ceiling. Thousands of small flowers instantly bloom. Each one holds a tiny sparkling grey wolf, howling a quiet flutelike song. They spring forth from the blossoms, fluttering through the air like little dog angels gliding on invisible wings.
****
With each passing day, White Coyote's thick mange skin becomes healthier. Her fur grows more and more, until it reaches the fullness it was years ago. Her little coywolf puppy becomes a tiny mirror image of herself and every day the puppy grows stronger from its' mother's milk. When White Coyote is not grooming and feeding her pup, she is teaching the coywolf how to stalk fish while remaining unseen. She shows her daughter the importance of eating the fruit that grows here. She explains to her puppy, "The seed is where all life comes from."
Coywolf is a beautiful puppy. She has large brown eyes, and a constantly wagging tail. Her paws are small and dainty; she walks carefully around the cavern investigating all things with her pink sniffing nose. The butterflies tease the puppy, seeing how long they can hover near her ears before she snaps at them playfully. They always escape before it is too late.
The ant people, always watching, whisper sweetly to the coywolf puppy; telling her some things she cannot understand.
"Learn to number every bone in your body."
Coywolf laughs and tilts her small head to the side. She thinks this will be a tricky task.

"Soon you must go above ground with your family little one, you're almost ready. The men you will encounter above ground are similar to us Ant People in some ways. Even now they are busy tunneling beneath our cavern with their tools. So you will see how they are different and the same."
A loud rumble shakes the cavern causing the far side wall to shift like a stage curtain being lifted upside down. Coywolf clings tightly to her mother's side, trembling.
"Look forward little one, there are many beautiful things to see." White Coyote licks the top of her daughters head, coaxing the scared puppy to open its' eyes.
Coywolf obeys her mother. She slowly opens her eyes. Breathing deeply, she takes in the wonder of what is revealed to her; a beautiful night sky holding a shining full moon. The mother helps her daughter climb outwards. As they move towards the large opening together. Little grey stars float out of the cavern passing them by, while twinkling upwards to dance around the moon and form a shimmering cloud. We are free. I fly away from the cavern, through the sky and the clean spring air. Looking back briefly, I see White Coyote and Grey Wolf with their new puppy Coywolf standing high in the mountains. On the outside, Grey Wolf howls for a long time at the cloud covered moon. When Grey Wolf stops, the family can hear men screaming from the rubble-covered boomtown beneath them. "Rockslide!"
A few more boulders slide down, sealing the underground land along with the ant people back into secluded safety and forever separated from the outside world. Little Coywolf's eyes grow large as the slowly rising sun introduces himself to her for the first time. Coywolf howls a high-pitched greeting to the new day. Both Mother and Father join Coywolf in singing.

Chapter 6
New Beginnings

Rocks from the slide settle into new places blanketing the town. I land atop a large boulder. Beneath me, a woman named Anya is trapped, along with one hundred and thirty-three other men, women and children the mountain has claimed for itself. Anya cannot see or move her strong arms and legs, yet somehow she is still alive. Wearing only a light nightgown, she lays tightly nestled against her collapsed bed. Her home is crushed with rocks and pressing in at her from all angles, surrounding her body is heavy darkness. Anya remembers who she is and where she came from. She woke only seconds before the rockslide happened. She had heard the miner's screams and the mountain's roar.
As the rocks engulfed her home, she had no time to escape.
"I will not die like this." She utters to herself.
Anya has lived her life with one regret. I listen to her thoughts pass, as she gets ready to move on to the next world. When the time comes I will guide her along. She is different than the others who have died and are dying in this town. I will find out what is unique about Anya. I sit atop my rock quietly getting comfortable. Beneath me, Anya begins to count things that I must wait for her to let go of. She slips into her memories.

*

At six years old Anya took a boat from Russia to Canada along with everyone else in her church family group. They had left their homeland by the thousands as political refugees, having faced persecution for being pacifists. A famous Russian author had sponsored the group's move to Canada.

The White Coyote 45

Her parents had told young Anya they needed to leave Russia, because they desired to live a life free of interference. When her family arrived in Canada, all her people were given raw land to farm and make their own. The women of her sect were very tough. They had a reputation of out working the men. Most English speaking Canadians made fun of the women in her group constantly for not being as dainty as women should be. Anya remembers her mother ripping up several newspaper articles in tears.

"We welcome them onto our farms. We share our knowledge openly and they ostracize us, calling my sisters fat and ugly."

Anya's genes and strong upbringing have left her everything but fragile looking, however her feelings and sensitivities are just as highly tuned if not more astute than many of the bullies who looked more delicate in appearance.

When Anya was nineteen, a traveling trapper named John came to her family farm in the prairies trying to sell furs and secure some work. He had mistakenly dismissed Anya's mother, addressing only her father with his inquiries. In turn her mother almost dismissed his business outright.

"We are all family here boy! We do not need outsiders to get us furs or mend our fences."

But the young man persisted, changing his tactics; he spoke candidly to Anya's mother.

"I have the best furs. And I will work as hard as you do."

Anya's mother smiled at the young man's confidence. Her father took a look in the trapper's bags. After heavy negotiation, her mother offered the boy dinner along with one nights lodging in exchange for a fine spotted pelt that Anya's father had chosen for her mother.

"Now you will look finer and be warmer than any of the silly girls in town who do not know how to run a plow!" Her father spoke these words while holding the fur like a coat around his wife.

Anya and her parents had let out a hearty laugh.

"HA! HA HA HA!"

John the trapper had looked confused for a moment, until he caught on. Competing was something these people only joked about.

Awkwardly John the Trapper tried to laugh along, still hoping to make the deal. Noticing the young man's discomfort and wanting to ease his uncertainty, Mother spoke up loudly; "It will make a soft bedspread anyways!" Mother's statement caused Father to laugh harder as John turned a ghostly white. Although John considered himself "well travelled" for his region, he had never seen a married older woman who spoke so boldly. His own mother would never have dared in saying such things. Realizing he was not breathing and his hosts were staring at him, John quickly decided that even if things were different about these people, all was still well. He found the boisterous Russian woman's charm contagious. Taking a deep breath in, John began laughing along with her. Anya found John very attractive when he laughed.

It did not take long before Anya and John had fallen in love. He spoke to her as his equal or better. Together, they planned on leaving her parents' farm and making a new life with fortune for themselves, gold panning. Anya had been excited at the prospective adventure. John left first, making his way towards the Rocky Mountains, with high hopes of earning enough for a wedding before Anya joined him permanently. Anya stayed at her parent's farm, saving her money and selling vegetables to townspeople. In less than a month she was on a train, following in John's path. She was heading towards a new frontier. She would be the first woman on the BC gold rush scene.

Sadly, John passed away shortly before Anya arrived in the Rocky Mountains. John's friends gave her a small share of John's earnings, along with their condolences. The Men expected her to return home immediately, but Anya stayed. She became very successful staking out the best claims. She earned enough in gold to trade for and purchase many supplies. After a short time, she owned a thriving store. The people of this small boomtown did not know what to make of the never married businesswoman, however their need for supplies often outweighed their need to have things be in a certain order.

Often during the night and sometimes in the day, Anya felt a presence watching her.

The White Coyote

The "presence" was nothing Anya had known how to explain. Even if she could have explained what she felt, she had no one to tell her highly strange story to. The feeling had started when she was panning for gold in the river; on the second day she had arrived. She knew some of the men had plotted to run her off, but something had stopped them and she didn't know what. When she had walked from the river to camp, her path always had trees broken down as if a giant bear had angrily passed down that way only moments before her. At night, in her tent she would hear men lurking outside, approaching drunkenly with ill intentions. Yet before the men ever reached her, they would hurriedly scramble in an opposite direction. She could not explain it. After only a few failed attempts at harassment, the male pioneers gave up bothering Anya.
Years past and Anya grew to be rich and successful, but she was lonely. At night in her cabin, Anya would see a shadowy creature outside who was not a man, but definitely not an animal either. Anya always knew when the beastly creature was near because he had a strong smell about him. In her opinion his natural musk smelled a lot better than the wives, who would wear the cheap French perfume she now sold at her store. She began leaving apples and beer outside on a stomp for the creature who watched over her, in thanks for his protection. Sometimes, the beast would leave her twisted up branches which she hung as wreaths upon her door. No one in town spoke of this, perhaps no one else noticed?
**
Heavy rocks threaten to squish Anya's last breath from her body. Anya's only regret in life is not getting to know the Sasquatch better. She wishes he would come to her now.
***
White Coyote, Grey Wolf and their pup all marvel at the rising sun. Coywolf sits timidly with her parents. She takes in all the sights and scents of this spring day. Chaos ensues the town below them. A smell like garbage that has been shit on, and set on fire blows towards them on the breeze. The odor is so strong; it competes with the sun's brightness and works in forcing most eyes closed. Coywolf becomes fearful, moving to crouch between her father's long legs with her hackles up. She is shaking.

This new smell in the air is so rancid. A howl unlike any dog's breaks the chaos into a stilled silence.
Although my words will not do the noise which Sasquatch makes any justice, I will try to paint an accurate picture of this sound for your mind's eye. You would have to be there, hearing it to understand the intensity. His howl is louder and fiercer than fifty hungry wolves. You can hear it in your bones. When he finally stops, your ears pulsate with aftershocks of deafness. Confused by internal silence ringing inside you. Your senses break their normal relation to the natural world; you become frozen for a moment. Fear is the first feeling that radiates through you, enlivening your numb body. You have a strong urge to run, because you could never fight this. You seek to hide from whatever did that to your ears, but you are curious. You stay where you sit, with eyes squinting. You want to see the Sasquatch for yourself, so you fight hard against your panicked instinct to curl into a ball with your eyes shut tightly and forget this ever happened.
Looking into the distance a large, orange figure appears distinct from the forest. The figure moves very fast in a way that looks stressed and easy at the same time. He is coming directly towards me, while I perch atop the remains of Anya's home. He looks mad. I quickly leave my post, flying upwards. The large ape like creature, bounds across more boulders now beneath us. He is sniffing the air wildly. He stops himself directly below me, standing where I sat only moments ago.
The Sasquatch begins digging and hurling rocks wildly in all directions. I have to move higher away from the air pocket I coast on to avoid getting hit by anything. Not immediately finding what he seeks, he stills himself for a minute. Frustrated, he screams out in agony, knowing he will have to go deeper if he is going to find Anya. Time is slipping away. Soon it will be too late. He does not give up. He resumes digging less frantically now, gingerly placing the boulders up and out of the hole he has made.
Removing another large rock, his rough, hairy hand brushes against Anya's bare, bruised leg. The Sasquatch grabs Anya by her ankle, lifting her out from under the debris. Flipping Anya right side up, he plants hundreds of kisses all over her face and neck before tossing

her over his shoulder. He leaves carrying Anya. He walks along the same path he came from this time with ease. He makes giant strides over the fallen rocks with a grace and stability, retreating into the forested hills with his woman.

Grey Wolf coaches his shaking pup out from under him. The surviving towns people looking all around take notice of the dogs. Grey Wolf ushers his family to follow the Sasquatch into the woods. This is not the first time Grey Wolf has met Sasquatch. He considers Sasquatch to be his friend. As soon as they are safe from human sight, Sasquatch hurls a giant log towards the little dog family. It smashes into many pieces on a rock beside them.

"What is this!? Grey Wolf barks, surprised at Sasquatch's aggression.
"You're scaring my woman! Go back the way you came Wolf." Sasquatch's tone is harsh and unfriendly.
Anya has been clutching Sasquatch's back fur tightly in her hands for fear of falling. She loosens her grip. Her big beast man and the wolves are talking to each other in a way she faintly understands. It sounds sort of like screaming gibberish. Anya wants to be part of the discussion too.
"I'm not scared." She yells.
Sasquatch groans feeling very irritated, however he is the most intelligent of the forest dwellers and always reasonable. Listening to his woman and looking at the cowering, fluffy puppy, he smiles. Relaxing his stance, he lowers Anya down onto her own feet. She slips her hand into his.
"You can stay right here, until you are ready to move on." He tells the dogs.
Anya looks past the relieved family of wolves in front her. She can see down into the whole valley from where she stands on the mountain. Her mouth drops open. Where once stood a busy town are now just large boulders. The road is gone, the train and tracks are missing. The undead townspeople look like tiny ants digging and running around. She hears them screaming out loved ones names.
"Sarah!"
"Todd!"
"Ryan!"

Anya can't watch the horrific scene beneath her much longer, she drops her head down. The peoples' screams in heartbreak and pain hurt her heart deeply. No one calls out Anya's name. With Sasquatch, she turns her backs to the town forever. They walk away further into the hills. Sasquatch makes small strides, taking special care not to drag his fragile woman.

Little Coywolf charges up behind the pair, nipping at Bigfoot's giant ankles. Suppressing a laugh, he turns around and bellows a load roar at the naughty puppy while thinking;

What is cute about a puppy left unchecked will get a grown wolf killed.

With his free hand Sasquatch punches the tree beside him. It breaks instantly.

"Pass this line and you will regret what happens."

Coywolf lowers her head. Her ears go flat back. Turning defiantly, she lays down on top a cliff face, overlooking the partly destroyed village beneath and pouting for having been disciplined. White Coyote and Grey Wolf lay down as well, showing respect for Sasquatch's authority. Coywolf does not lay still for long. As soon as Sasquatch and Anya disappear further into the mountains. Coywolf goes stomping and jumping all over the hill. Mimicking how the Sasquatch moved. Coming near to the broken tree line, Coywolf attempts to roar as he did- but her bark come out high pitched and squeaky. She uses a front paw to swipe a still standing tree. To her surprise, the tree stays standing and little Coywolf hurts her paw. Limping and whining she goes to White Coyote who consoles the silly puppy.

The family rests, curled up together in the afternoon sun. Coywolf falls asleep, tucked in safely under her mother's front leg. I watch the little pup from my perch in a tree. She recognizes my presence, and lets out a little growl to let me know it. I change my sights, now looking down at the town in the valley. The men there are busy, trying to clear rocks away from where a road and railway used to be. It seems an impossible task. Eventually they will give up, and decide that building a new road and railway atop the wreckage is much easier than trying to work through it.

The White Coyote

The townspeople are busy all day long. They constantly hammer and bang their tools in a loud desperate rhythm, trying reclaim what is now gone. They make it hard to for me to get any rest during daylight. When the sky becomes dark, the people will sleep and mice will come out. I will hunt then.

Beneath the rubble, the old town is full with people who died. The ghosts of men forever trapped, under the rockslide grow more upset with every passing moment, not knowing they have passed into another unstable dimension. They move through rocks not seeing what is all around them and scream out to living people who will never answer them. A few of the ghosts who are not particularly attached to this town wander off down the long desolate highway, seeking a place they hope will be better. The majority of dead are stuck like glue to their surroundings and will angrily continue on for all eternity seeking to fix the unfixable.

The sun sets and the sky is swallowed in blackness like a disease. Two hundred barely living men approach the town on foot seeking to replace the men who have perished. They walk downcast looking starved and lonely. They speak a different language than the survivors of the town. Cautiously the workers climb over the rubble, making their way towards the still standing homes. Most can't see the ghosts beneath them, but they feel the wicked taunts hurled at them by the deceased.

"Go back to China!"

"We got enough men here, and a fine railway already!"

"Leave scabs!"

The eerie echoes of bad vibrations and recent trauma brings the men seeking work chills in waves. One man leads the rest forward. A leader in charge of the whole group, his only distinction is that he stands apart and in front of the others. His skin sags from his emancipated frame just like the rest of the hungry men he leads forward.

"Be calm!" he tells the other workers in their own language. "We are almost at the foreman's house."

When they get to the largest home still standing in what remains of the town. The leader knocks on the door, while the others wait.

The leader speaks both Chinese and English excellently, but rather than use his skills to communicate with ease- he has learned that most townspeople do not offer him much respect regardless, and far less when they feel threatened by his abilities. He speaks to the foreman with a put on heavy accent, purposely mispronouncing common words.

The foreman appears pleased and tells the leader to instruct the rest of the workers to set up their camp away from the town. This lack of hospitality is no different than any other of the many work sites this group has been on. The usual overwhelming sense of offence from being subjected to this type of rudeness is put off for tonight. The workers are pleased to be setting up their make shift, shanty homes out of range from the ghosts and ghouls inhabiting this place.

Grey Wolf is hunting high in the hills under a black and starry sky, looking for sustenance to provide for his family. White Coyote and Coywolf snuggle together in the open, sparsely treed hills awaiting Grey Wolf's return. White Coyote wants fish. Her sleepy noise searches the air for good smells as she drifts from wakefulness. She dreams of picking up faint odors of a wolf looming in the distance, the time she first met Grey Wolf and catching many rainbow fish.

Clouds overtake the sky above, hiding the stars and still sparkling with electricity. Coywolf is awake and wanting to explore. She creeps and squirms from her mother's side, peering down towards the town, intrigued by the sounds coming from the new camp being set up and the new smells accompanying that. Inching free from her mother's sleeping grasp, she inches further and further away. She peers down the hill, away from where her mother rests. A deer path is visible, Coywolf goes to the edge and looks over. The incline is long and steep but doable.

A loud noise rumbles throughout the night sky, scaring little Coywolf; her feet go squirrelly beneath her. She wants to run back to her mother, but it is too late and she is already tumbling down the hill. Lightning flashes illuminating everything. The little white puppy narrowly misses trees and jotting, jagged rocks as she slides out of control down the hill towards the camp. Rain falls hard, making Coywolf's plummet faster and more slippery.

Chapter 7
Pack Mentality

Coywolf tumbles to the bottom of the steep incline, away from her mother in a momentum she cannot stop, she rolls into the back of a worker's tent, coming to a complete stop in a tangled mess of raw material. A man touches her through the canvas that's tightly wrapped around her muddy, wet fur. She tries to jump- the material restricts her. She's completely confined and can't see. She growls and cries out. Her cry is answered by a long howl. It sounds like her father's voice but it's not. The man on the other side of the canvas retreats his grasp on her as he lets out a terrified scream. "Demons!"

The rain soaks Coywolf, pooling up inside the material bondage trapping her. A large puddle forms, making it difficult for her to breathe. The camp grows noisier. Guns fire. Coywolf struggles to breathe through her nose, smelling only wet dog. Large paws scratch outside the canvas. Suddenly she has air. An unknown, large female alpha wolf picks Coywolf up by the scruff of her neck. The workers who survived this surprise onslaught of ravaging wolves run off quickly abandoning the camp, while the few unlucky remainder who became too feeble during last year's winter to escape are eaten alive by the wolves. Their cries of anguish are terrifying. Coywolf hears her father howling in the far distance. Rain continues to fall. The big wolf mother drops Coywolf with her nine puppies in a thicket of bush, growling a warning at Coywolf to stay put. The nine puppies are much larger than Coywolf.

"You smell funny!" The biggest and bravest male puppy of the nine barks at Coywolf. The others giggle feeling playful, as they pounce around Coywolf.

"It shouldn't be here with us, it's not even a wolf!" The largest female puppy speaks, while turning her nose up in disgust.

"Tell us what it is sister?" The pup's stops playing to wait a response.
"It's a mange coyote you fools! Stay back or she will make you sick and mange too. Mother probably put it here for us to guard until she's ready to eat it."
A smaller female puppy chimes in "Mother says, she loves all puppies no matter what kind of dog it is. Mother would never eat a puppy, even if it is a mange coyote."
Coywolf had never felt bad before about being part coyote. She had never thought her mother and father were different species, only that males were big and strong and females are small and clever. Looking at the big female puppy hurling insults, Coywolf comes to a realization; perhaps her mother and father choose to be certain ways, not because they are wolf and coyote or male and female, but to create balance with in their family. Coywolf looks past the nine big puppies now viciously nipping and growing at her. The workers camp is in shambles. Everything around her is destroyed. She can hear men screaming but their cries do not permit any mercy from the hungry wolf pack engulfing these people and everything in this place whole.
The Alpha female returns with a slab of fresh meat for her children. The nine puppies descend upon it, wrestling each other for every last piece. Coywolf has never eaten meat. All her meals so far have come from nursing at White Coyote. Starving, she tries to get in on the food, but the others will not let her have any. They wall her out with their backs.
When the last morsel of food is devoured and with their bellies full, the pure wolf pups fall asleep contently. Coywolf sits awake in the rain, whimpering out for her own mother, feeling alone, hungry and frightened. She sees something that has no smell and makes no sound peering at her with glowing yellow eyes from behind a tree. Coywolf's hackles go up and her little tail tucks between her legs. The thing disappears and then peeks out again from around another tree further away. Crouching and creeping forward on her belly, Coywolf shakily follows the thing away from the sleeping puppies. Mud from the rain mats her white coat. She continues to move forward.

White Coyote and Grey Wolf run down the hill toward their missing puppy. The rain has masked many smells including the pack of wolves who await them, and the exact direction Coywolf has travelled. Reaching the bottom of the hill, they easily see their pup with luminescent fur creeping across the ground. They greet each other with kissing licks. White Coyote and Grey Wolf are so relieved to find their child that they do not scold her for wandering off. The three are feeling such a happy bliss from being reunited that nothing else seems to matter and time stands still for a moment.

Grey Wolf takes his eyes off Coywolf, to see what makes the noise around him. His hackles go up as he takes a protective stance, growling he does his best to shield White Coyote and Coywolf from the large pack of ravenous wolves surrounding them. Grey Wolf is scared. The wolves tighten their circle around the little family. Grey Wolf frantically changes positions trying to protect both females in his care at the same time.

A large wolf steps forward "Stop. All of you right now!" her tone is low. She growls to her pack, giving no mistake to whom is in charge. The Alpha female directs the wolf pack to back off just a little from the terrorized mixed breed family of three. Stepping forward, she directs her words at Grey Wolf.

"Nephew, why do you trespass upon our group with this Coyote?" Grey Wolf recognizes the leader as his mother's sister from many years ago.

"Our puppy wandered off. We came to retrieve her. We mean no harm."

The Alpha female nods, acknowledging she hears Grey Wolf's reason. Loving all puppies as every wolf does, she decides to make him a fair offer.

"You would be wise to leave your pup with us rather than let it be raised by that abomination of a dog you have cowering beside you as your mate. I have already adopted her as my own. You and the pup may join my pack. You are family by blood, my nephew and rightfully that makes the puppy mine. Step aside and I will kill the mother."

The White Coyote 57

"What good can become of a pup without it's natural mother? She is still nursing. She has been in your care only a few hours and look, she is already famished. Your milk has dried up and your puppies are much older than little Coywolf. In a pack this large, there will be no scraps leftover for her. She is too young to fulfill the role of an omega." Grey Wolf speaks his words sincerely, while trying to appeal to the Alpha female's heart.

"True she is scrawny and appears just as foolish as her coyote mother, but if she stays with us she will have the chance to become a true wolf." The Alpha Female's response isn't the answer Grey Wolf wanted. He does not give up, reasoning further;

"And what if my little Coywolf cannot keep up with your puppies' hunger and strength?"

"Then she will parish as nature intends. It is very simple nephew. The only choice for her is to become a strong, large wolf." The alpha female's words chill little Coywolf and White Coyote to their bones. There is no reasoning with this wolf. Bad things are coming. A physical conflict will be inevitable. Grey Wolf's instincts are divided. On one hand he is drawn to protect his new family, on the other hand he shares more genes and heritage in common with the wolves threatening them. Looking back and forth, he does not know what side to choose.

The pack widens their circle of entrapment around the family, as the alpha female moves in closer. Grey Wolf makes his choice, relaxing his position between his aunt and his mate. Coywolf skitters under White Coyote's legs for protection, terrified both for her mother and herself.

The alpha female makes eye contact with White Coyote, the look She gives White Coyote is filled with generations of hatred and malice wolves have held against Coyotes. There will be no peaceful resolution here.

Moving ever closer, the Alpha growls to Grey Wolf; "It is a wonder you did not kill this rejected dog yourself when you came upon her. Tell me nephew, why did you continue to let her live? She is not one of us and never will be." The alpha female's words taunt White Coyote and confuse Grey Wolf. Little Coywolf growls out from under her mother.

The alpha female circles the family, creeping in ever closer. The crowd of watching wolves is excited for inevitable blood. Before Grey Wolf can completely dissolve into the pack, White Coyote hisses a command to him; "Take the pup."
Growling, White Coyote lunges forward at the alpha female, darting over Coywolf, closing the gap and taking the former aggressor by surprise. Being twice the size and much better in strength than White Coyote, the alpha female had not expected such a brave advance. The alpha female had thought White Coyote would run, never the less, she opens her large jaws and prepares herself to rip the coyote's head off. White Coyote dips between the alpha female's legs. From her low position, she turns onto her back in a mock submissive position.
"Please, just let us go on our way." White Coyote whines.
The alpha female shows no mercy, laughing instead- she is enjoying the coyotes begging and the feelings of power that come with it. Easing her guard and losing focus, she feels her victory to be secure. Her eyes shut slightly as her mouth waters in anticipation of the fresh kill that is about to occur.
Using teeth and claws, White Coyote rips into the alpha's soft under belly. Blood and guts cover White Coyote and the mud beneath. The large wolf stagers, collapsing on top of White Coyote. White Coyote flails her legs and turns her head back and forth- biting harder, while shredding and serrating the aggressor's wounds as she kicks the dying body away from herself.
The pack recedes from around White Coyote, except for one male who felt he was second in line to rule the pack. He too challenges White Coyote, but her cunning is too great for the beta male. He falls in the same way his leader had. Exhausted, and with the threats nullified, White Coyote lays down panting. Grey Wolf releases his grasp on Coywolf, allowing her to go back to her mother. The puppy is hungry and needs to feed. The pack mourns the alpha female's death lifting their heads high to howl out into the night. When their song is done, they devour their fallen leader's wounded carcass quickly without joy, purely on instinct. All but two puppies partake in the last meal. A female wolf pup watches the sad scene stoically.

The White Coyote

Coywolf sleeps soundly, nestled safely against White Coyote's thick fur.
*
I hoot in warning to the dogs, from my perch in a tall tree. All this noise and movement has attracted unwanted attention from the townsmen. They are hungry for more money and approach with their guns ready. A dead wolf is worth a bounty of one hundred and fifty dollars, paid by the government. I continue to hoot in alarm, but the wolves do not understand me. Most are full and drunk on meat. They sleep peacefully. Little Coywolf and White Coyote hear me. They awaken. They attempt to wake up the rest of their new large pack. Although she killed the alpha female, many of the more passive aggressive wolves in this pack pay no attention to White Coyote's authority. They laugh at her claims for group retreat, making no move to escape what approaches them.

White Coyote pleads with Grey Wolf to leave. At first he only yawns and dismisses her. He too mourns the loss of his aunt. After extensive begging from his mate, he slowly gets up to take full charge of the situation. He coaxes some of the wolves who will listen to him, to follow him, however many wolves stay where they lay. Ten, nearly full sized adult male beta wolves walk behind Grey Wolf, in a large quiet line. Of the alpha female's nine puppies, the most daft swears vengeance for her mother. Some of the others make their choice based on being terrified of being left alone. All follow White Coyote. Hearing the first of many gunshots this evening, the new pack stops dead in their tracks while making their way over the rockslide's boulders. Lying down amongst the ghosts, the new pack formed of twenty-three rests for the evening.

I watch the men in their foolishness. They have caused much pain, disaster and destruction since their arrival here. I become lost in my thoughts as I look down from my perch at them. *It would've made more sense for the townspeople to have properly accommodated the workers. Going out shooting the wolves that targeted the sickly, displaced and put out workers after the fact seems as though they baited the wolves. Trying to shoot the remaining wolves at the immigrant worker's camp is a wasted effort. They can't kill them all and are only creating more. In any wolf pack, no matter how large, only the alpha pair will breed. Tonight, the men's shots and encroachment has dispersed one big unit into four smaller packs each will have new breeding alpha pairs. The men are only creating more problems for themselves. Perhaps it is not ignorance but a greed for bounty dollars that drives them? Man is the only animal who will seek out another healthy thriving adult animal in its prime to kill, while showing no altruism for their own kind.* Too disgusted in man's flawed "logic", I fly off into the dark night sky, leaving man to his own devices. I follow after the newly formed pack being led by Grey Wolf.

During daylight, the new pack restfully waits out the hot sun in comfort of shade. At night the pack follow Grey Wolf eastward under the slightly illuminated ghost trail left in the starry evening sky by the previous day's sun. In a not so long ago time of their ancestors; wolves roamed freely. I soar on warm winds above the pack. After three days moving along, the mountains become small behind us. We are moving through more and more man habitat. The land is stretched with farmer's fields and domestic animals, places where the sheep and cows are fed but wolves are despised. The further we go east, the more dangerous our lives become. We have no choice in crossing man's path almost daily, although myself and the wolves would prefer not to if given any say about our journey's path.

The sun is rising. White Coyote is exhausted from caring for the large wolf pups, who are relentless, wild and untrained. They listen to nothing White Coyote tells them and don't learn from her cunning teachings in the least. The puppies contribute nothing to White Coyote and take all they can, greedily. It is different than raising her own little Coywolf, who takes heed of the knowledge passed on. Before joining with the wolf pack, White Coyotes remembers the early nights with her pup ending in restful contentment. Now, nights end only in strain and exhaustion.

**

Finding refuge, the group lays down in the shade, behind a dilapidated old barn. This place has been abandoned for years and has become weathered. Overgrown, weeds engulf the barn- forgotten by human sight but still on their territory. The wolf pups are hungry.

The White Coyote

Although their diets contain mostly meat, the puppies are not proficient hunters yet. When allowed to participate in a hunt, they do more to foil things than help.

The nine pups demand grows bigger for larger shares of each kill. The few kills the pack has made over the past week, and the slight smell of man constantly on the air has left the adult providers weary and feeling run down.

Restless in their hunger a pair of full grown, beige brothers, along with Grey Wolf and his cousins sniff around the old barn while White Coyote and the pups try to rest. Previously, the nine wolf puppies have never experienced hunger so extreme as their fast growing bodies feel now. In their old larger pack, the nine always had ample shares of the food along with four stand-in mothers available to nurse them. This feast or famine lifestyle has not been best for them.

The wolf puppies have reverted in their behavior, trying to nurse on White Coyote while she feeds her own little Coywolf. At first White Coyote allows the nine to feed but they are greedy and overwhelming. They push Coywolf to the back, not allowing the little one to get any milk. White Coyote lifts Coywolf by the scruff of the neck and climbs to the rafters of the barn out of the wolves' reach. Here she can to feed her small pup in peace. The nine cry and whine for White Coyote to come down. They jump at her and make clumsy attempts to follow her tricky climb, but they have no success and eventually give up. The strongest of the puppies joins the adult males in scavenging around for food.

Grey Wolf's natural instinct is to avoid man, mostly following elk and deer trails to seek food has left him confused about being at this barn. It still holds the faint stink of man. In every direction around him, man's smell is present. Sometimes, it comes stronger on the wind. There is now where else he can lead this pack for the time being. They will need to bring down a large kill and fast, or starvation and mange will get the better of most of them. Grey Wolf shivers, trying to shake off this thought. Putting his nose to the grass he picks up the scent of an animal.

He barks softly letting the rest of the hunters in his pack know.

I hoot to Grey Wolf from my perch atop the barn, but he has never paid any heed to my warnings. He must lead the hunters of this group to find food or they will all parish. There is no wild game left in this part of the land, only livestock.
'If this puts us in direct conflict with man, at least those of us who remain will have the strength to move towards a safer place.'
His reasoning is as sound as it can be, given his circumstance. There are no other options left. Following the scent out from the barn, the males spot a lone cow on the horizon. Her black and white spots are illuminated in the suns light. She is old, slow and can't hear or see well. She appears unconcerned with the wolves' approach. They come up cautiously on the cow verifying; yes, she is alone and has strayed from the rest of the herd when put to pasture. Being fatter and slower than the other cows has made her a prime target for the hungry wolf pack. The two male beta grey wolf brothers circle the cow. Still, she does not appear scared. She holds her ground, ignorantly. Mooing out across the fields, to no one in particular while continuing to chew the cud in her mouth.
Grey Wolf lies still on the grass with the nine pups beside him, watching as the Beta Greys tighten their strides around the cow and test her for weaknesses. The excitement is too much for one brave little wolf pup. He bounds to his feet and runs full out at the cow. The cow does not move. The little puppy circles around the back of the cow and nips ferociously at her hind legs. The cow bleats out in pain. The rest of the wolves move in, taking the cow down. There is nothing graceful in how the cow manages her huge weight. She does not stand a chance in shifting purposefully out of danger. She crushes the grass beneath her with heavy stomps. The impatient wolf pup's front paw gets trampled by the distressed cow. Crying and whining loudly, he limps back towards the old barn. He seeks comfort from White Coyote. The rest of the males enfold upon the poor cow, tearing pieces from her live moving body. The cow is still making steps. She tries to get away while the dogs hang off her. They bite into her ample flesh. Grey Wolf descends upon the gruesome scene to end the bombardment. He latches onto the cow's neck and twists his sharp teeth deeply. The cow falls, giving the hunters their fill.

The White Coyote 63

I fly back into the barn, perching myself on the rafters where White Coyote had previously sat with Coywolf. Looking, down I can see she has returned to nurturing her own pup as well as the adoptive wolf pups as well. The wounded pup comes limping and whining towards the group. The smell of fresh blood in the air has gotten all the pups, including Coywolf excited. The injured puppy talks about the beast that trampled his paw.
"It put up a huge fight, roaring at us, but we won!"
All of the wolf puppies except the injured one and Coywolf go running out into the farmer's fields searching for the kill, using their small sensitive noses to lead their hungry bodies through the tall grass. Growling sharply White Coyote calls after them.
"You must slow down pups! You are not even looking with your eyes to see what you are heading into!"
They do not listen to White Coyote, continuing on quickly towards the promise of a meal. White Coyote leads Coywolf towards the smell, following behind the fast moving puppies. She tells Coywolf to be cautious and alert for predators like bear or man. The injured little wolf stays alone in the barn licking his hurt paw. His feelings of excitement and hunger have left him now, overcome with pain and a wounded ego. His pride hurts worse than his paw.
Grey Wolf, along with the pack's adult members guard the remains of their kill, keeping the first excited pups who arrived on the scene at bay until White Coyote approaches with Coywolf. Grey Wolf barks and snaps at the beta's who are unwilling to share the cow, forcing them to obey and retreat, allowing the hungry mother along with her pups to partake in the great feast. White Coyote and the pups eat until their bellies are full, while the males lay around snarling and chewing over large pulled bones. White Coyote tares off a small bone for the little injured pup who stayed at the barn. Leaving the rest of the pups in the Grey Wolf's care, she returns to the barn.
"You only brought me a little bone?" The hurt puppy growls at White Coyote from behind a haystack.
"Do not be ungrateful." White Coyote snarls back at the puppy. "Come out from sulking, and eat, this bone will help your bones heal faster.

The hurt little wolf, twists his face is despair and sadness.
"It hardly has any meat on it at all. Mama would've brought me meat. Coyotes know nothing about anything- other than being mange."
"That is a foolish thing to say to someone that has brought you a gift, but if that is your opinion- you do not need to eat it. I am also hungry, so I will eat it up."
"Nooooo!" The hurt pup angrily swipes the bone from White Coyote. She does not mind, as this was her plan anyways.
Night sets in. The pack drags what remains of the cow's dead body into the open barn continuing their feast. They look like house dogs, happy and well feed gnawing on bones. Some of the older wolves are lounging and chewing lazily, while most of the pups frolic about happily. With too much energy, eight wolf pups drift out from the barn onto the field where under the starry sky, I am hunting for mice and frogs. The Little wolves are curious about my actions and watch me with their heads tilted sideways. Getting distracted, they bark, wrestle and nip at one another. They are scaring away my dinner. It takes a long time tonight for me to spot another mouse with the puppies being so disruptive.
I must move further away from the pack if I am to get any food for myself. Soaring through the dark sky, I descend upon the mouse before it knows what happened. I prefer to eat in silence away from the noisy puppies. I swallow my meals whole. I can't have any stress to my system while extending my throat in this way. Wolves will never understand about finer manners of silence. After watching them eat the cow live, it is a wonder I have an appetite at all. Their jaws are much stronger than my beak, yet I always manage to kill my prey before consuming it. Lost in these thoughts and allowing my body to do the work of regurgitating the indigestible pellets from my catch, I am brought back to this world as my eyes register two faint lights approaching from the distance.
Readying myself to take flight, I rev up my wings internally without moving outwardly. This brings my body temperature high enough to take flight. I must get a closer look at the lights. More than likely it is from men carrying the lanterns- but how many?

The White Coyote

Before I move, I am pounced upon from behind. The stupid puppies have followed and surrounded me, yet they are not playing. An orange/grey coloured wolf pup nips at my tail feathers.
'Wolves would kill their own mother's spirit.' I think angrily as I fight the puppies off and fly away to a treetop above the approaching men. White Coyote, sensing danger, leaves the barn. She comes to collect the pups sternly. Seeing the lanterns in the distance, she growls lowly and speedily ushers the wayward pups back towards the barn.
Four men walking the field below me talk amongst themselves. Two men in the lead carry their lanterns high. The oldest man is the father of the others with him. He owns this land, and trusts that every blade of grass on his land is for him to control and bend as he chooses. I don't like their mentality. If these men had followed the way the first people had lived here before them, we would all still be living freely. These men have come to retrieve their missing cow. The father is blaming the oldest son for allowing the cow to wander so far.
"Not like old Elsie to miss her evening milking Pa. I thought she'd return on her own for sure. She's probably on her way back now. She's just slower than the rest because of her foot rot." The eldest explains with a nonchalant attitude.
The father turns and swings suddenly cuffing his eldest son upon the ear. "You are always full of excuses boy! If you had put a bell on her- like I told you to weeks ago, we wouldn't be in this mess now." The father will not have excuses.
The younger boys who are following behind snicker. I swoop down and around behind them, gliding slowly and noiselessly on the wind. The youngest son senses my presence. He stops dead in his tracks; gulping hard, he turns around searching for what he will never see.
"Elsie!?" He calls uneasily into the night. I fall back to give them more room. You never know about these men with their guns. And even the scared youngest boy one holds a riffle shakily at his side. Noticing his youngest boy has held up the procession, the father begins to demand answers. "You hear something back there Todd? Because, I didn't hear nothing. Did anybody else?"
Beginning to feel foolish and unsure of what to think Todd answers his father. "No Pa. I just got a feeling."

"Oh...Feelings eh?" The father says sarcastically lifting his eyebrows and making an ugly face for his boys to see by the lantern's light. He has always held an extreme revulsion and disgust for his youngest child. The way the boy had continuously clung at mother's apron strings and acted more like a girl had set the father into uncontrollable rages many times.
The three young men begin laughing and turn their teasing from the eldest towards the youngest. The middle son pipes up. "You better run back home to Ma! She knows all about dealing with them feelings..."
They all laugh except the youngest whose face has gone hot red. Luckily the light is not on him. I find their laughing contagious. I shriek out my best hooting laugh along with them. The men become quiet, as I continue on gliding around them and cackling.
"What in the Sam Hill is that!?" The father asks to no one in particular.
The pack of wolves at the barn has stopped their peaceful feasting and relaxing. Grey Wolf smelled the men's odor on the breeze before White Coyote returned with the wondering pups. Slowly, the wolves exit the barn one by one. Heading eastward away from the men. The injured wolf puppy limps along, doing his best to stay close to the front of the pack with the other puppies. Some of the betas do not want to leave their pieces of cow bones, so they linger and growl possessively. As the men come closer, the wolf's instincts get the better of them. They leave their food to avoid running into the men. The betas move fast to catch up with their pack evading the men completely.
Some of the puppies grow over excited as they slip away. "Why don't we just eat em, like we did the last people?"
"Yeah I could eat one, I'm not full yet."
"It's no fair leaving our bones for them..."
White Coyote hushes the rowdy pups, and keeps them moving along. "We don't attack men, unless there is absolutely no other choice. And even then, it is unwise. You pups may have been ruined by tasting human flesh before. It's not something that normally happens or will ever happen again. Those men your old pack attacked were weak, dying and most of them did not have the guns."

White |Coyote continues her advice, though it falls on deaf ears. "For us wolves and coyotes it is always better to flee from man, than to engage him in a fight. No interaction with man is best, and anything he has made or has his scent on is dangerous."

The injured pup barks snarky comments at White Coyote. "Coyotes are stupid and nothing like us wolves. You know nothing and you are not my mother. I'm not listening to you." He lifts his nose in the air, prancing forward faster while limping slightly, he follows Grey Wolf more closely near the front of the line. The other pups fall in around and behind him growling arrogantly at White Coyote while ignoring her warning. All except Coywolf, she stays silently beside her disrespected mother. They all head further eastward away from the approaching men.

The pack travels for many weeks, crossing rivers and streams until the mountains filled with gold and coal become only memories in the back of their minds. I follow the pack across many horizons, yet things are becoming uncomfortable for me. The wolf puppies sabotage my hunting with their ruckus play all through the night. They drain White Coyote until her body becomes thin once more, yet no matter how they try, nothings can break her spirit.

Coywolf has a hard time getting her share of milk and food. The nine wolf pups are larger, stronger and greedier than she, however little Coywolf is more cunning. She manages to stay alive, but barely. White Coyote has a difficult time getting her share of the meals although she is the alpha female of this pack, most of the wolves including the nine pups do not care for or respect her. The nine pups grow larger than White Coyote.

***

We come to a place where the land is as flat as shale rock, and the horizons stretch on forever. There are no forests here, and not much free flowing water either. This land holds only farm plot squares, man has divided this space up with fencing to hold in their crops and animals neatly. The wolves will have to be very clever at all times to get through this division of land, barns, and houses undetected. Once, many years ago this area was a good hunting ground, but today there is no game. The Wolves are hungry. There has not been anything to eat for many nights in a row now along their journey.

The wolves are growing desperate. This sprawl of land completely taken over by man is too large for the wolves to cross without any substance. They know better than to kill mans' cows and sheep, however starvation is taking hold, and the pack is running out of options.

The sun lightens an early morning sky, casting orange and pink hues across the fields of grass, barns and houses. The nights are shorter in this far stretching flat land, although night usually becomes longer in the mountains at this time of year. The pack take refuge from the sun, hiding behind bundles of large square hay stacks. Perching on top of the hay pile, I use my talons to dig down into it. I form a small nest around myself. Beneath me, in the stacks some mice are rustling about in their dens, the tiny creatures are settling into sleep. Like us, mice prefer to stay hidden during hot days. I listen intently for a moment. I shuffle over to the left slowly. A family of twelve mice is directly beneath me, snuggled in together. I wait until I sense the last wakeful and small mouse has settled itself. I hunch low on my feet, my legs and small neck coiling into my round body. When I was still in my mother's nest she would chuckle at my cuteness in this position. I remember the reflection of myself in my mother's eyes; I was a fuzzy oval. Coming back to the present, with all the strength in my body I jut my legs down into the hay, quickly bringing both legs back up to me with handfuls of mice. Squeaking and wiggling in pandemonium, most but not all of the mice escape my grasp. They go scurrying down the haystack running for their lives in terror. Closing my grasp tighter on the two remaining within my talons, I kill them instantly. I swallow them whole.

Coywolf and White Coyote wait with anticipation, open jaws and tilted heads for the waterfall of mice tumbling down towards them from atop the pile. They each snap up a few before the wolves realize what is happening. The grey betas growl and snap at both mother and daughter, angry that they did not get first dibs on the tasty morsels. Hungry and jealous, the nine wolf pups whine nastily. They nip at White Coyote fiercely, to let her know who is entitled to first servings with in this group.

"We are starving, and the mange coyotes are taking everything! It's not fair!"

The White Coyote

Coywolf is so small; smaller than White Coyote was when she was a puppy that age. Picking her pup up gently by the scruff of the neck, White Coyote climbs the hay pile awkwardly to escape the wolves growing rage and hunger. Grey Wolf ignores what is happening; not feeling inclined to involve himself in what he sees as only a petty pack squabble. He agrees that the lesser coyotes should not have taken first dibs on the mice.

The wolf pup that was the bravest before his paw was crushed by the cow now whines the loudest, faking pain and distress. He screams for White Coyote to come back down to him. Lifting his grey snout into the air he sniffs for her, hoping to pull the mother's entire essence back to him. With his nose stretched up towards White Coyote, he picks up a scent similar to his adoptive mother's smell. At once he sneezes, clearing his airways to properly take in the new scent. Lifting his noise high, he smells the air again. He turns his head in the direction the new scent has come from.

Reading the pup's body language, the other wolves in the pack follow his gaze to a tuft of grass in the distance. A small red and beige face with alert dog ears is peeking out. Realizing it has been spotted; it disappears down into the grass. All at once the wolves form a circle around their new prey. Grey Wolf leads the drawn out attack. White Coyote and Coywolf stay atop the hay trembling. They can smell the unfortunate coyote's blood is kin to their own blood. Little Coywolf shivers, tucking in close to her mother. "They had the taste of man's blood on their tongues, and now they're eating a coyote like us. We will die in this flat land with these wolves, one way or another."

White Coyote gently licks Coywolf's quivering back, soothing her she says;

"That may be so, and you are not wrong to question how they behave, however it is more likely that their foolishness will cause their own deaths before it causes ours. Stay alert my little one, and also try to remain calm as well."

Trusting her mother, Coywolf snuggles in closer. She buries her nose deep into White Coyote's fur, hiding it from the offensive smell. Her ears cannot block out the sounds of the Coyote's cries as the wolves devour him alive.

The wolves take their fill of the unfortunate lone coyote, leaving only a few small bones. Day turns to night. White Coyote jumps down from the hay pile. Coywolf follows. Her little legs are not yet strong enough, to withstand impact, causing her body to become a lump of unharmed white fuzz upon the ground. The wolves laugh at Coywolf's fall.

"Nice jump stupid." The large puppies bite at Coywolf while she is down.

Grey Wolf ignores the wolf puppy's bad behaviour dismissively. His thoughts are completely un-empathetic towards his own daughter. *She will need to grow stronger to survive in my pack.*

White Coyote growls at Grey Wolf. She is upset. "You should offer better protection and support for our daughter! If you hate all coyotes then why did you make her with me? How long before you eat us too, my husband?"

Grey Wolf pretends confusion. Looking at his mate with large innocent appearing eyes, he tilts his head.

"What do you want? I cannot change the way things are?"

White Coyote holds his gaze, unforgiving. Her eyes become smaller as if to contain all the rage spilling from inside her. She says nothing.

After a moment, Grey Wolf lowers his head. He does not care to understand White Coyote's anger. He grumbles; "It is not wrong for the strong to do what we must to survive, this is normal pack mentality and it always works out for the best. Perhaps you are just hungry. You need to do a better job getting what you need instead of blaming the rest of us for your shortcomings. Understand this fact and I will take pity on you and your disgustingly weak puppy one more time."

Using his nose, Grey Wolf slides one of the small remaining coyote bones towards Coywolf. Coywolf jumps back horrified at this offering. She does not remember any of the feelings of fondness and safety she once felt from the pack leader. Grey Wolf growls at Coywolf. Knowing that she is outnumbered and not wanting her daughter's fate to be the same as the deathly remains in front of her, White Coyote thinks quickly. A standoff will not end well. She takes up the bone in her mouth.

The White Coyote

Bowing in forced thanks, White Coyote walks behind the haystack, with Coywolf following closely. Once they are out of sight White Coyote begins digging a hole in the ground. She buries the little bone.

Another restless day and night passes at the haystacks, uneventfully, before the pack continues following Grey Wolf east for many more days. White Coyote and Coywolf tail the large wolves from the rear being very careful not to crowd or become too close to the wolves. Three beta's march further back behind the mother and daughter, keeping them in line and snapping at their heels when the space between them and the rest of the pack becomes too great. Coywolf grows weary and sickly. She is no longer able to keep the forced pace. White Coyote carries Coywolf along by the scruff of the neck. She is afraid of putting her pup down to rest. The wolves force the Coyotes along, now ready to take advantage of any weakness without hesitation. White Coyote does not show outward fear. She keeps her head high while marching along with the ones hoping to kill her. She wishes for the pack of wolves she calls family to find something else to eat soon.

Continuing on further across a seemingly endless horizon, the pack comes to an unmanned field. It is filled so full with sheep that it looks like snow has fallen in a perfect large square of fluffy white. All the wolves' yip and bark with excitement, a few of the pups run quickly ahead, down into the huge sheep pen. The quiet, white field becomes marred with red splotches, barking dogs, and screaming sheep. Cautiously Grey Wolf smells the air before leading the rest of the pack down. Each of the twelve adult wolves takes down a sheep, with some killing two or three before they begin consuming what they can. The nine wolf pups are large, but still grossly unskilled at hunting. This is shooting fish in a barrel. The pups fatally injure many of the trapped, bleating sheep but do not inflict wounds great enough to bring any of their targets immediately down.

It has been many weeks since White Coyote has gotten any part of a hunt. She wants to take advantage of this opportunity to escape the wolves, however she knows that if Coywolf does not eat soon, she will die. White Coyote follows along behind the wolves' lead into the field of sheep.

I watch the wolves in their wastefulness from a safe distance, the way their chaos fits perfectly into this square box, that the men have set up. I see White Coyote cautiously approach a sheep that has moved away from the majority of the herd. Gingerly, White Coyote rests her pup on the grass near the fence and out of harm's way. Quickly she goes for the lone sheep's jugular vein. In a clean, quick kill it's blood spills onto the dry grass beneath. Coywolf lays on the grass watching her mother through sore half open, crusted eyes. The nine large, greedy wolf puppies see White Coyote has found success in quickly taking down a sheep. They feel entitled to her spoils. Rushing towards White Coyote, the wolf pups nip at her fiercely, in threats to take over her kill, even though there is plenty of other sheep. They are now as large as White Coyote, and with all of them working together to block her, she must abandon hope of her own belly being satisfied. White Coyote's heart pains her worse than her stomach as she looks on at her little, weak pup laying listlessly away from the rest, just where she had left her.

White Coyote barks angrily at the nine wolves hogging her take down. Charging forward and standing her ground, she rips a hind leg from the dead sheep. The wolves bite and tear at White Coyote as ferociously as they do the dead sheep. White Coyote does not give up. She pulls the hind leg away from the snapping wolves, however, this prize costs her a large piece of her right ear. White Coyote does not concern herself with this injury. Breaking free, she drags the leg over to Coywolf. White Coyote has to encourage her sick puppy to eat. This takes time. She must rip off small pieces of meat and place them before the little one. After only a few hard won bites, Coywolf begins to look brighter and slightly better. Coywolf stands on her own. Hungry now, she moves towards the full meal her mother has provided. Both Coyotes begin consuming opposite sides of the leg bone. The pair finishes their shared meat while the wolves continue on in with their consumption and slaughter. The pack spends the rest of the day and night sleeping in the pen alongside the remainder of many hurt and frightened sheep.

Coywolf awakes, feeling herself again. She looks at her once pretty and sweet mother, and realizes her mother is no longer the same.

The White Coyote

White Coyote's eyes are now deep set. Her once smooth faced is deeply lined. One of White Coyote's teeth has cracked away from too quickly gnawing on the inedible hard bones the wolves had rationed to her along the trip. Worst of all, her mother's right ear is shredded to tatters with a large piece now missing from it. Coywolf questions her mother.
"What happened to you? Who hurt your ear?"
"The wolf pups have become larger and more savage than I." White Coyote answers while turning her head to the side, hiding her new deformity from Coywolf. Looking out to the field full of carnage, she whispers,
"|At least I am doing better than most of these sheep."
Coywolf follows her mother's gaze throughout the pen. Many of the sheep lay dead with only small pieces missing from their bodies. The few sheep who remain intact huddle together fearfully in a far corner. The inequity of this, as well as the loss of her mother's ear is too much for Coywolf to accept.
"We could've eaten these sheep for months taking one at a time! There would've been plenty for everybody! It makes no sense that the wolves destroyed most of them. Only the wasting diseases that make things sick can eat them now. We came upon this food by chance. We may never see this many sheep again!"
White Coyote nods in agreement with her child. "Things need to change."
"Then why don't we just leave right now mother? The wolves will not even notice."
"Now you are being foolish. Once they've had their fill of sheep, they will track us down. We can't end up like that other coyote. Although they came across him by chance, they now have a taste for our blood in their mouths that they won't forget it. Besides that, we are headed in the same direction as the wolves anyways."
Coywolf looks sadly across the field. She sees me pecking at the already decaying sheep carcasses. "Spending this much time around wolves has turned the Owl into a vulture."
"The only reason the Owl does that is to clean up. The dead sheep attract predators and sickness. Owls are wise, and she is helping us get through this.

You cannot judge her for staying near us and doing what she has to." The sun disappears. A dark evening sky paints itself above the sheep pen, as if a great invisible hand colours meticulously, slowly shading the sky darker. Grey Wolf approaches with three adolescent female pups following closely behind him. White Coyote shakes her head sadly. She had always believed that wolves mated for life. The bitch closest to Grey Wolf snarls, lowly scolding White Coyote for her unapproving gaze.

Grey Wolf glares back at White Coyote; "I have no responsibility to mate for life with a Coyote. You have grown arrogant. You're foolish to challenge my authority, rather than keep your place." White Coyote lowers her head in submission.

'I'm no longer sure what you wolves want with me and our daughter, who you would just as soon allow to die."

Grey Wolf speaks. "You are obligated to remain with my pack and whatever I determine your function to be- is not your business. You do not have any right to question me, or superior wolf traditions. We leave soon, to continue east. Man will come to look at his sheep eventually and we do not want to be here when he does."

Coywolf watches silently, as White Coyote lowers her head in a show of respect.

When Grey Wolf leaves earshot, Coywolf confronts her seemingly defeated mother. "How can you let him treat you like that?"

"Hush little one. I understand Grey Wolf's logic, even if his reasoning has damned him. True, I once thought he loved me, but I know wolves share more blood amongst themselves than with Coyotes. I am no fool, even though I was only filling time along his path to becoming Alpha. He has taken from me only some of my time in this world, but from him I got you and that is the greatest gift I have ever received. It matters not at all to me what he thinks or says now. You and I will survive."

****

The pack moves on, heading eastward and following Grey Wolf's lead- leaving mass destruction of livestock in their wake. After many days traveling, doing as they please and moving on before getting caught, they come to a town with an ocean breeze drifting on the breeze into their astute noses.

The White Coyote

The Wolves eye's draw the town's edge taking in everything from farms, a mill and small houses- to the forest all around the outside. Grey Wolf has a choice to make; he must decide if the pack will cut through the little farms full of delicious sheep, or take the long game path around the outskirts staying inside the forest's safety. The pack stops moving forward, all members look to Grey Wolf for a decision. He gazes down the long game path, smelling for fresh travelers. He catches the scent of nothing recent. He looks to the fields, licking his lips at the sight and scent of not closely guarded sheep. He moves forward towards the farms. Watching him and not following, White Coyote shakes her head in disgust. "Has greed finally gotten the best of your common sense? You choose to endanger us all even though we have a chance at peace and safety? If we don't try to remain hidden from Man, he will kill us all for interfering with his sheep."

Grey Wolf raises his head in pride. "My pack is big and strong. The nine wolf pups have grown large and fierce under my leadership. You are wrong to question me lowly coyote. I have made my decision. We'll all cut through the farmer's field and eat some of their sheep...Unless you want to keep arguing me because if that is the case, we can gladly eat you first." He snaps his jaws at White Coyote.

The pack surrounds White Coyote and Coywolf. White Coyote becomes silent and lowers her head. In submission she lays down, rolling over onto her back, to show them, she does not want to get eaten and has dropped all opposition. Pleading, she tries to makes it clear that she is no threat and that she will follow Grey Wolf's lead. Some of the pack moves in on her swiftly, hopping from side to side growling and barking at her. They haze her, an attempt to scare her- however none approach too closely. The wolves all remember how the cunning coyote had once killed their alpha female. Coywolf crouches low beside her mother. In truth the wolves are more frightened by White Coyote than she is of them. With Coyotes, they never know what to expect, and they hate her for that. The wolves tire of asserting dominance- backing off just a little, they allow White Coyote to standup and rejoin in ranks with the pack as they move along on a path set by their leader.

Beta wolves nip at White Coyote's and Coywolf's heels, forcing the pair to perfectly fall into line. Grey Wolf stops the groups' momentum. He sniffs the air. He smells meat in the distance. The wolves divert their path slightly, walking towards the delicious smell. Cautiously, the wolves come upon fresh cuts of livestock meat, with no hints of nearby man on the surrounding air, the meat however does have a slight whiff of man to it. Grey Wolf puts his nose against one of the many slabs.

"It is not man meat, although it has been handled by man recently. Perhaps they saw us coming and ran off in fear." He boasts before sinking his large teeth into the steak. He swallows a big piece, no chewing. He addresses the pack who drool while waiting their leaders consent and approval. "It is perfect meat, and there is plenty for all. Man has left us an offering; there is no harm in consuming what he gives us. We will all eat well tonight my family." The pack moves in, consuming the gifts, but White Coyote and Coywolf hang back.

I cannot be certain about White Coyotes thoughts at this time, as I watch the greedy pack from my perch on a fence post. I can tell you, dear reader that White Coyote and little Coywolf are the only members of the pack with blood still flowing to their brains rather than stomachs at the sight of the steaks. We will never know for sure what caused the mother and daughter to hesitate. Whether it was the vicious conditioning inflicted on the pair by the wolf pack that caused the two to wait for the others to be satisfied before taking a share for themselves, or if White Coyote and Coywolf waited because they sensed better than the wolves that they were being baited in a trap they could not see. I like to think both factors contributed to their choice of not indulging. Personally I would never eat anything man has tampered with, gift or not.

Making quick work of every last morsel and not caring weather or not the coyotes ate; the wolves consumed their doom happily. The pack took rest at this spot near the town, giving their stomachs a chance to digest the feast. Coywolf and White Coyote lay down too and with empty stomachs- they did not sleep. I soar on a soft breeze towards the tree line, waiting for the pair in the woods. As the sun sets, I hoot twelve times into the wind.

The White Coyote

A truck engine rumbles in the distance. White Coyote and Coywolf rise, their paws steadily beneath them. The wolves will never awake from their poisoned slumber. Leaving the wolves behind them, the pair walks towards me. Upon reaching the forest, they duck out of sight behind a large tree. Both sets of coyote eyes peer carefully around the tree, staying hidden. We watch as a group of five men walk towards the dead wolf pack with guns drawn.
"Be silent." White Coyote warns Coywolf.
"I know mom."
White Coyote works hard to keep herself from laughing. Her pup has grown up into a beautiful smart Coyote with a sharp attitude. Two men in the distance begin speaking amongst themselves.
"Fifteen fine pelts, each one catching us one hundred and fifty bucks a piece in bounty. That aint bad at all! Bahahahaha! We'll be living it up this Friday night, that's for sure."
"I don't know Bob, by the way folks have been talking about all the damage done in other towns- I'd have thought this pack had fifty wolves, not fifteen. Doesn't seem like this could be all of them."
"They ate all fifty steaks though didn't they? I'd say this is the hungry pack we've been after"
"I'm not convinced Bob, there could be more in the forest hiding"
The men all gaze towards the forest. White Coyote and Coywolf watch, while staying hidden. A chill runs up the men's spines, as I hoot into the night.
"Ah well, if there are more in the woods, we'll catch em all tomorrow eh. I'll bring the truck in closer to load up this lot anyways."
The man called Bob returns with his truck. Soft snowflakes begin to fall. The men collect up the wolves' lifeless bodies. White Coyote and Coywolf continue deeper into forest, still headed east. They make a den, and manage to stay hidden for a short time. When the coyotes sense the men have followed their tracks in the snow too closely, they move further east. The pair keeps east, until the land goes no further. They come to the icy, stony edge of the partially frozen ocean. A scent blows on the wind behind the pair, whispering to White Coyote and Coywolf that man is quickly closing in on their heels.

There is nowhere left for us to go but further out. The coyotes jump off the edge, splashing where they land and swimming without hesitation through the cold, wavy ocean water until they can pull themselves onto a large block of ice. I follow them gliding easily on the salty breeze. When I need rest, I sit beside them. We catch and eat every sea bass who approaches the surface too closely checking out our ripples. We float happily out to sea, on a block of ice.

The End

Epilog
The Island

The mound of ice we travel on bashes, colliding with an area of completely frozen solid ocean. I fly up and see, we have come to a large island. White Coyote and Coywolf walk across the water on thin ice. As we get closer, the island gets bigger. We see boats frozen in time. On land, red, blue and yellow houses and farms are placed randomly and in sporadic clusters. Nothing is spaced and fenced so tightly and uniform as Man had kept the dwellings on the mainland. The island people feel different. Climbing up a steep hill, the coyotes find a large bowl of dog chow near a bright red barn. Man is close by. A male golden retriever barks to them.
"Hey! What type of dogs are you?"
White Coyote walks on, ignoring the foolish dog and his chow. She wants nothing more than to distance herself from the stench of any men. Coywolf is curious about the dog and stays a moment to speak with him.
"We are not dogs. We are coyotes." She says proudly.
"We've never had coyotes here before!" The golden retriever is excited to meet new friends. He wags his tail enthusiastically.
White Coyote waits for her daughter in the bushes, silently weary of being so close to a man dwelling. She wonders how the dog can live in close proximity to man.
Coywolf makes an offer to the dog "Come with us, this island is so big, that we don't need to crowd man."
The friendly dog tilts his big yellow head to the side, his ears perk up and his large paws prance beneath him excitedly. Enthusiastically he barks his reply "Okay! I love going places!"
An island man opens his back door just in time to see his dog (for the last time) running away forever into the woods with Coywolf. "Gus!" the man screams, trying to recall his dog, but it's too late. Gus and Coywolf have fallen in love.
Approaching a roadway, Gus becomes leery.
"Master has rules about these, he's always yelling to me 'OFF THE

ROAD STUPID DOG!'"
White Coyote continues, walking onto the gravel and dirt. She stops in the middle of the road, turning to look at her grown pup Coywolf standing on the edge of the road with the big dopey dog called Gus. "Come along. We can't go around all this, so we need to cross. Stop dilly dallying." She assumes the role of Alpha, barking commands at the younger pair. Thinking in her head;
These two are the future. My place is no longer in this world.
A fast moving truck, packed beyond full with logs to burn and sell comes speeding around the bend. White Coyote does not move. She looks through her own eyes for the last time, seeing the mirror image of herself in Coywolf. The truck thumps loudly over White Coyote's now limp body. The driver carries on.
I fly away, towards the setting sun. White Coyote is with me, as we leave the new pair and the confines of our earthly bodies forever behind us. The hearts of our eternal souls' rhythm beat with never ending contentedness knowing Gus and Coywolf will have many puppies together and live mostly happily ever after.

HISTORICAL FACTS
~ According to the Newfoundland Department of Environmental Conservation; Newfoundland has a higher than average occurrence of White Coyotes.
~ The first documented sighting of the "Spirit Dog" in Newfoundland was made by a pet owner who stated that his dog (a male golden retriever) ran off, never to be seen again with a white coyote. It is assumed this event began the population surge of this new species.
~It is believed, the original white coyotes made their way as far east as possible by traveling across ice, after deforestation and human consumption of natural habitats on the mainland forced them to do so.
~The last laughing owl also known as whekau or white faced owl was found dead in 1914 at Bluecliffs Station. It is currently extinct, although unconfirmed sightings have been reported since that date.
~Extinction of the laughing owl was directly caused by human interference with the natural environment. Persecution.
~ 17 000 Chinese people were shipped to Canada between the years 1881- 1884, by the Canadian Pacific Railway to work as cheap labourers. Many people died due to sub par working conditions and poverty.
~ In the year 1905, over 100 residential schools existed in Canada run by the Roman Catholic church. Indian people were forced to submit their children to the schools, by the Canadian Government. An average death rate of 40% of the children attending residential schools at that time is recorded.

Melissa McLarty is a Wife and Mother. Growing up on the mountains, she developed a love for the outdoors. Currently living in beautiful British Columbia with her family. She is a passionate nature lover and holds great respect for sustaining our environment. Every summer, her garden is full of sunflowers- which happily attract bees.

Made in the USA
Charleston, SC
17 April 2016